MOTHERKILLERS

Portrait of Ignáz Füllöp Semmelweis by A. Canzi, 1857.
By kind permission of the Semmelweis Museum, Library and
Archives of the History of Medicine, Budapest.

MOTHERKILLERS

John Piper

Book Guild Publishing
Sussex, England

First published in Great Britain in 2007 by
Book Guild Publishing
Pavilion View
19 New Road
Brighton, BN1 1UF

Typesetting in Baskerville by
Keyboard Services, Luton, Bedfordshire

Printed in Great Britain by
CPI Antony Rowe

A catalogue record for this book is available from
The British Library

ISBN 978 1 84624 087 4

To Odete

Contents

Acknowledgements

This book could not have been written without the help, support and encouragement of many people. In particular, I would like to thank my wife Odete who has graciously tolerated me when I have been present but my mind has been elsewhere.

I wish to express my appreciation and gratitude to:

In Budapest – at the Saint Rochus Hospital, Mrs Eszter Hoványiné, mathematician and information advisor, Dr János Szabó, medical superintendent, Dr Kausz István, clinical director, Dr Josef Gabanyi, outpatient superintendent, Dr Susan Turi, head of the obstetric department.

At No 1–3 Apród Street – Mr Benedek Varga, Deputy Director, Semmelweis Museum, Prof. Michael Németh-Csoka, clinical chemist.

In London – Mr John Gross, writer and journalist, Prof. Edward Randall, physicist, Department of Chemistry, Queen Mary College, University of London, Miss Ann Adams, oncological nurse, Mrs Helen Crisp, Prof. R.M. Kirk, surgeon, Mrs Naomi Pritchard.

In the Algarve, Portugal – Mrs Diane Parkinson, for typing and preparing the manuscript, Mrs Manuela Vale, artist, Mrs Linda Chester, nurse, Mrs Brigitte Dübal, German translator, Dr Laszlo Biritz.

I obtained information from pamphlets, papers and

journals but was especially helped by Gy Gortvay and I. Zoltán (Semmelweis), K. Codell Carter (Ignaz Semmelweis) and A.J.P. Taylor (Hapsburg monarchy). I thank these and other scholars and apologise if I have inadvertently bent some of the facts. That is, of course, my responsibility.

I especially wish to thank Carol Biss and her colleagues Susannah Foreman, Joanna Bentley and Janet Wrench at Book Guild Publishing for their encouragement and expertise in producing *Motherkillers*.

Prologue

In 1845 a killer stalked the great maternity hospitals of Europe, North America and probably the rest of the world. Mothers and babies were slaughtered in great suffering on a monumental scale by this mass murderer.

The name that was given to the assassin was puerperal fever. (The word 'puerperal' means 'of, or caused by' childbirth.) It was also, at that time, known as childbed fever.

Within a few hours of giving birth the affected woman experienced the hot and cold shivering attacks familiar to flu sufferers. This was rapidly followed by severe abdominal pain and a foul vaginal discharge. All of these symptoms became speedily worse with associated profuse sweating, headache, continuous shaking, called rigors, and respiratory distress.

At this stage of crisis some patients spontaneously started to improve and recover. However, many progressed to circulatory collapse and multiple organ failure leading to death.

Today we know this is the picture of septicaemia, which is infection and eventually pus in the bloodstream. In 1845, no such words or concept existed.

This was a time before the great discoveries of Pasteur and Lister. It was also a period in which a scientific approach to medicine was emerging using careful and detailed observation. Statistical analysis was being born but bacteria and antiseptic were yet to be the common words we hear today.

Within the Vienna General Hospital of 1845 puerperal fever held the same terror for the mothers in the maternity department as elsewhere in the world. The hospital was, nevertheless, regarded as the centre of medical excellence in the Austro-Hungarian Empire. There was keen competition among doctors to work in all the departments.

In the maternity department there was a young Hungarian doctor struggling to gain a foothold on the bottom rung of the obstetrics career ladder. His name was Ignaz Semmelweis. He was a gentle, kind and industrious young man with a cheerful disposition and a sense of humour. However, he was outraged by the suffering of women in childbirth and especially by the appalling ravages of puerperal fever.

There were many theories held by prominent figures in the world community of obstetricians at that time regarding the disease. It had been recognised since the time of Hippocrates. He had described the condition of *Lochia febralis*. Lochia is the name given to the normal vaginal loss after childbirth, which lasts a few days.

The ailment had remained unusual in the Vienna hospital until 1810. This coincided with the more widespread practice of post-mortem examinations.

Among the more ridiculous theories of its cause was that breast milk travelled the wrong way, passing in, rather than out.

The most popular hypotheses to explain puerperal fever centred around the atmosphere from which 'something' affected the patient. This was extended to miasmic (noxious vapours) and telluric (of planet earth) influences.

All this seemed highly suspect to Semmelweis. He,

therefore, set about a meticulous programme of clinical and statistical observations. He worked tirelessly for many hours, days, weeks, and eventually, years. He did indeed discover the cause of puerperal fever and a method for its prevention. This culminated in 1861 in the publication of his book *The Aetiology, Concept and Prophylaxis of Childbed Fever*.

In the intervening years and subsequently he suffered abuse, humiliation, obstruction and deeply offensive accusations both verbally and in print. Nevertheless, those hospitals that did introduce his methods saw a dramatic decline in the incidence of puerperal fever. This included hospitals in Vienna and Budapest.

General acceptance of his observations, principles and recommendations did not take place in the worldwide medical community until after Ignaz' painful and tragic death in 1865. His name is little known outside his native Hungary. Nonetheless he was a giant in the history of medicine.

This book seeks to promote a wider knowledge of the man and his achievements. It has been done through the eyes of a fictitious young woman called Charlotte Weiss.

The story includes both real and imaginary people. However, as much as possible, historical accuracy has been observed and any errors are regretted.

Although these events occurred a century and a half ago they still have a resonance in today's world, for example the plague of MRSA (Methicillin resistant *staphylococcus aureus*).

Had it not been for Ignaz Semmelweis many of our great, great, great grandmothers would not have survived childbirth and some of us would never have been born.

Ignaz Fillipe Semmelweis (Ignác Fülöp) was born in the Tabán area of Buda on 1 July 1818. In those days Buda and Pest were individual cities with their own mayors and separated by the great river Danube. Buda was the capital of Hungary.

Tabán was the bridgehead of the Danube's only boat-bridge and a busy commercial centre populated largely by Germans and Hungarians.

Semmelweis' father József ran a grocery at 1–3 Aprod Street, which burnt down in 1810 and was rebuilt. He married Terezia Müller on 7 June 1807. They had ten children of whom Ignaz was the fifth. There were three girls and seven boys, the last of whom was stillborn.

Ignaz was born in the rebuilt house that still stands today on the west bank of the Danube and has been converted to a medical museum dedicated to his great discovery, his family and medical practice of the time.

He had a happy childhood, was industrious at the local catholic school and fond of animals. He moved on to university in 1837 and, in keeping with his father's wishes, studied law. However, he changed to the faculty of medicine after one year.

He graduated in 1845 but this coincided with the death of his mother and he returned to Pest for a few weeks.

He was accepted shortly afterwards as an external postgraduate (aspirant externist) doctor in the first obstetric clinic of the Vienna General Hospital and remained there until 1850 when he returned to Pest. During this time he made his great discovery concerning the cause and prophylaxis of puerperal fever. He encountered many difficulties.

He continued his work in Pest from 1850 until his death in 1865.

In 1857 Ignaz was married to a raven-haired beauty, Maria Weidenhoffer, aged twenty. It was always a happy marriage in which professional problems were not allowed to intrude. They had five children, but the first two died in infancy. However Margit, Bela and Antonia brought great happiness.

Maria lived until 1910 and in 1906 attended a ceremony of the unveiling of a memorial plaque to her late husband at the house where he had been born.

The 1932 Hungarian 4 fillér postage stamp in bright ultramarine bears his portrait. The 20 fillér stamp in deep rose red portrays Franz Liszt.

1

Charlotte

19 June 1845

A particularly vicious swirl of wind swept down the Vienna street. It whipped the rain into horizontal sheets that penetrated every possible place of shelter.

Charlotte pulled her cloak tightly round her swollen aching belly and cursed the rotten sod who had forced her out into this bloody awful weather in the middle of the night.

She had flopped into bed three hours ago, already exhausted after a day scrubbing the floors of the lodging house, which paid for her shabby room on the top floor. It seemed as though her heavy eyelids had only just dropped shut when she felt the warm waters between her youthful thighs trickling back to the crack separating the cheeks of her bum.

The pains had started almost immediately. First a gripey twinge like she had had three weeks ago, with a bout of the trots. It only lasted a few moments but five minutes later it returned, stronger and longer. The third time and she knew the baby was on its way.

She had dragged herself out of bed, thrown the worn purple coat she had inherited from her poor dead mother around her shoulders, stuffed her feet, which were still

1

stockinged, into her ankle-length, lace-up black boots and crept out of the room. At that moment another spasm gripped her. She paused at the top of the stairs until it was over.

She hurried down the four flights of creaking boards but saw no one. She let herself out of the high wooden front door and into a really foul June night, more like Vienna in March.

Dressing had not been a problem; she had been too clapped out to get undressed when she went to bed. The layers of clothing seemed to give no protection against the biting gusts of wind and rain.

She set off along the dimly lit street. Many of the oil lamps sprouting from the walls of the tall houses had been blown out by the fierce wind.

She had passed only two buildings when another savage cramp drove her into a doorway in a vain attempt to seek shelter until it passed. Squatting down she rested her arms on her knees and drew deep breaths. The driving rain lashed her face.

Charlotte had two more roads and a long boulevard in front of her until she reached the Vienna General Hospital. In fine daylight it would have taken her twenty minutes but now it felt like a walk halfway round the world.

At last the pain eased and she struggled up on to her feet and started walking again.

Twice more she stopped; it seemed to be getting worse much faster than that old cow of a gin-soaked nurse had told her. She had been the only person to talk to when her tummy started to get big. The woman lodged in the room next to hers and had young women visitors who shouted and screamed before they left. They never returned.

Now the spasms changed; she had an irresistible urge to push and felt her vagina stretching. This time, crouched down in front of a massive gate, she instinctively knew the baby was forcing its way into this cruel, cold, sodden world.

She heaved with all her might and put her hands between her thighs and felt the head, then shoulders and little chest slide out of her. Finally the whole new human being was free of her body. It cried.

She stopped panting and breathed more slowly, resting back against the thick iron bars of the gate. She scarcely noticed the cold or the wet, even when a coach full of late-night revellers rattled past spraying even more water on her ... and the baby.

The baby, the baby – what now? She lifted it up and started to wrap it in her skirt that was now loose above her knees. Then she stopped; there was something, a thick slippery worm sticking out of the child's belly.

She ran the fingers of her left hand along it while clasping the precious bundle in her crooked right arm. She felt it go between her thighs and up into her body. She pulled on it and it didn't come away from her. She dimly remembered the old crone from the next room telling her about the cord leading to the afterbirth.

Without really knowing why, she tugged at a loose thread and yanked it free from the hem of her sodden coat. She wound it twice around the cord with slippery fingers and tied a knot one-handed, as best she could.

Gathering up skirts and infant in an untidy parcel she stood up, the cord tenting up the front of her bloodied petticoats. She wore no knickers, which was a bonus in the circumstances.

Once more Charlie headed towards the hospital. There was no pain now, only urgency. She desperately needed care and shelter for both of them. She hurried on over the greasy cobblestones turning into the last street that led to the boulevard with the hospital at its end.

She remembered little more until she found herself

leaning against the massive oak door that led into the Vienna General.

It slowly gave inwards and she staggered forwards and collapsed in a drenched heap on the tiled floor. There was no more rain.

2

Retained Placenta

'What have we here?'

'Another street birth, I shouldn't wonder.'

The two stout elderly women looked down at the heap of soaking clothes, mother and howling child sprawled at their feet surrounded by a rapidly spreading puddle.

They were the night orderlies, Ida and Gisela, dressed in long grey dresses of rough wool and covered by dirty white aprons. Untrained, they were there to sort out whatever came through the doors at night and point it in the right direction.

This might be to the correct hospital department or, for drunks, fighting whores and other troublesome riff-raff, straight back out into the night. They were tough and strong but kindly. They were experienced and worth far more to the hospital than the pittance they were paid.

Ida bent down and swept Charlotte's sopping hair off her face. She was pale, her skin cold and teeth chattering. 'The poor lamb, she's half dead.' She lifted the swathe of skirt and baby but was halted by the tightening cord. 'Gisela, fetch the midwife, there's a problem here.' Her colleague bustled off.

Ida knelt down and lifted Charlotte's head on to her ample thighs after releasing the baby back into the mother's arms. She gently touched her cheek. 'What's your name, love?'

'Charlie,' came the whispered reply.

'That's a boy's name.'

'It's really Charlotte. Please, what's happening?'

'Gisela's gone for the midwife, you're still attached to the baby.' Ida rubbed her cold cheeks with her rough hand, but it was done with tenderness. Loud footsteps on the wooden floor echoed down the corridor to the tilestone entrance.

'What's all this, then?' The small thin-lipped midwife in a long blue dress and apron reached down to the baby. It started to cry.

Charlotte was so cold and bewildered she scarcely noticed the midwife take some thread and a knife from her apron pocket, tie the cord twice and cut it between the two knots. She took the child and the two orderlies lifted the mother to her feet.

'She can come in, the cord hadn't been cut. It's the first division on duty tonight. Follow me.' Charlotte, dripping water and a few drops of blood staggered after the little nurse carrying her baby.

They turned into another corridor, this time covered with glass, the rain, which had started again, was beating against it now and running down in rivers. At the end they came through double wooden doors into a huge dark room barely lit with a few flickering candles in the centre. On either side Charlotte could make out the shadowy forms of rows of beds.

It was not quiet. 'Help me, I'm dying!', 'Shuddup! you stupid cow!', 'Aagh! the pain!', 'I can see the devil, he's come for me,' from unseen women.

Another female appeared and together she and the midwife peeled the sodden clothes from mother and baby. Standing naked in the gloom the cord hung obscenely between Charlotte's strong thighs. There was a steady drip of dark blood on to the rough boards.

She was dried with a rough towel and laid on the nearest bed. They covered her with two worn blankets and showed her the baby. 'It's a girl. Here, take her for a moment.' Charlotte took her daughter, kissed her forehead and exhaustedly handed her back.

Lying against the iron bedstead a strange feeling engulfed her, one she did not recognise but liked. For the first time in her eighteen years on the planet she was happy. She slept with a smile on her young face.

She woke to the sound of men's voices. 'Ah, the street birth last night.' Professor Johann Klein was tall, fat and snooty. He was surrounded by six younger men and a terrible smell. It was daylight. The smell reminded her of the rotting cabbages she had to clear out of the trench at the back of her lodgings, but it was worse, much worse. The men did not seem to notice it. 'Gentlemen, the placenta has not come away.' It was the fat man talking, 'What shall we do?'

'Bleed her,' said one young voice, 'An enema' from another, 'A cold bath,' shouted one more opinion. The great man, as he seemed to be treated, was not impressed.

'You all fail. Dr Semmelweis will tell us what to do.'

Until that moment Charlotte had not noticed the balding, slight young man standing at the back of the group. He had a fine, bushy moustache.

'Enquire of the midwife if she has attempted to express the placenta by compression of the uterus.'

'Exactly. Nurse Violetta?' The tone was imperious, from God himself.

'The night staff were too busy, we had two women die of the fever.'

Charlotte had not seen this new nurse before and with the room lit from windows high in the wall she saw a tall middle-aged woman with greying hair. Her light blue dress was covered by a white apron smeared with dark blood stains. She could also see beyond the gathering around her bed a huge long room with perhaps twenty beds along each side. She preferred to look around rather than listen to the discussion about her body.

She wasn't able to see the other women because of the men grouped around her but she could hear some of them. 'Oh gawd! I'm leaking that muck again down below,' a glum utterance to no one in particular. 'I can smell it, you dirty cow!' angrily. 'It's not my fault, it's that bloody priest and his bell,' came the reply.

The doctor and students didn't seem to notice the background cacophony. 'What next, Semmelweis?' boomed God.

'We should examine the lady.' The voice was soft and gentle.

'Examine, yes. This woman has given birth in the street. Are you married, girl?'

'No.' A whisper.

'Some lady.' The students dutifully smirked; Charlotte blushed and shrank under their contemptuous gaze.

'Get on with it.' The great man was becoming irritable.

'Heels together, knees apart,' commanded the midwife as she roughly pulled the blanket from the frightened and embarrassed mother. She felt her ankles grasped and pushed towards her bum. Charlotte resisted the hands pulling her knees apart. 'You must co-operate, girl.'

There was a threat in the words.

Resistance crumbled; her vulva was revealed with caked dried blood clinging to her pubic hair and the cord snaking out of her vagina. The students leaned forward and gazed at her plight.

Out of the corner of her eye she saw Dr Semmelweis circle round the students and furtively dip his hands in a bowl that rested on a wooden stand near the wall before he reached her right side. He touched her right wrist reassuringly.

He seemed to say, it's not good but it'll be OK. She couldn't see but felt him spread her vaginal lips which were still sore and push two fingers inside her. There was a stretching sensation with little pain but she suddenly wanted to pee.

'The placenta is partially through the cervix,' he announced to the gawping students.

'Let them all examine her,' proclaimed the Professor, 'an interesting case of cervical dystocia.' Semmelweis reluctantly stood aside and the first drooling student, unshaved, and shabby, dirty and smelling of rotting cabbages, roughly plunged his fingers into her. Now she felt pain mixed with revulsion. Seven times more she was invaded with no variation.

'Gentlemen, I will show you what to do.' The Professor swept the students aside and plunged a podgy hand followed by a still sleeved wrist into Charlotte. She screamed and writhed on the bed but the big man was powerful and peeled the afterbirth off the wall of her womb.

He pulled the placenta easily out of the vagina and held the raw meat dripping blood high above his head. The students clapped their hands. The great man nonchalantly tossed the purple oozing sponge into a nearby bucket with a splash.

The subject of the assault lay moaning, pale, sweating and unnoticed by the applauding apprentice medicos. They moved on after their hero to the next bed.

9

3

Fever

It was afternoon; a grey sky still lit the vast lying-in ward through the high windows, which occasionally rattled with a gust of wind.

After the medical procession had passed out of the room apparently bored following the excitement of Charlotte's bloody vagina and anguished screams, she had been given a bucket.

It was dirty, grey, smelly and half full of shit, urine and blood. Nevertheless, she had got out of the bed and naked, squatted over it and listened as she peed with clots of blood splashing into the swill.

Like the other women she had been given lukewarm soup, some bread and water. It seemed as though she was only allowed a minute before the dishes were cleared away.

A tall skinny woman with grey hair piled high on her head had entered through the huge door at the end of the room. She wore a long full-skirted black dress and rimless glasses perched precariously on the end of her nose. It became cold and quiet.

'I am Miss Irma Valerie, the controller.' She took a large black leatherbound ledger from under her arm, opened it and began to read.

'These are the rules for non-paying women.' The new

mothers, mothers to be and two whose babies had been stillborn turned their heads in unison. 'She loves this bit, the bloody bitch,' whispered Charlie's older neighbour.

'Be quiet,' Irma Valerie's rasping high-pitched voice held no sympathy. 'You are privileged to be in the first division of the Vienna General Hospital maternity department.'

'Since when is rotting to death a privilege?' The neighbour again, but much softer and apparently unheard.

'In return for the care and delivery of your baby you will have the following duties.

1. Make yourselves available for teaching students by our great doctors.
2. Submit to examination in labour, during delivery and afterwards.
3. Act as a wet nurse both for paying women's offspring and for the foundling babies brought in here.
4. Work, starting four hours after birth is complete, carrying the toilet buckets, cleaning the floors and helping remove dead women to the mortuary.'

Groans and muttered 'Piss off!', 'Go fuck yourself!' and 'You try getting pregnant,' greeted the daily litany of do's and don'ts. 'Her pregnant! That'd be another virgin birth,' confided the fearless neighbour, as the controller turned and left the room, heels clattering on the wooden boards.

Charlotte lay back. 'What the hell am I doing here?' she asked no one in particular. 'It's 1845, I've no money, no job, no home and my family is a girl six hours old.'

The windows rattled in the wind and the rain beat against them again. The wood-burning stove in the middle of the ward seemed to have gone out. 'Christ, it's cold.' In fact the room was quite warm.

'What's your name, dear? Mine's Alexandra.' The

11

vociferous woman from the next bed had climbed out and perched herself next to the shivering girl.

'Charlie. It was a joke by my friends because my boobs didn't grow until I was seventeen. My real name's Charlotte.'

'Feeling cold? It always happens afterwards. I should know, I've had seven, four living, including the one in here,' she patted her swollen belly. 'I can't think why it's so slow. The pains started three days ago and now they've stopped.'

Her companion was smiling: tall, thickset and friendly. Probably about thirty but looked nearer forty. 'I'll get you a hot drink.' She bustled off in her long brown woollen dress. She wore no shoes.

The new, first-time mother with no husband was reassured. There are some good people in this world, she thought.

Not like that rotten sod Rudolph Esterhaze who had promised her undying love and marriage when he caught her alone in her parlour maid's bedroom. He had slobbered kisses over her face and forced up her dress to have his way. Afterwards he never gave her a glance, friendly nod or a smile. He watched stony faced when she left the house, dismissed when the bulging belly could no longer be hidden.

Alexandra returned with a steaming cup. 'Lemon and barley, it cures all the aches.'

'Even the one in my heart?' Charlie laughed, she hadn't done that for a long time.

'Drink that and have a good rest, I'll do your chores. I don't think you'll be worried by the doctors, they've got a big congress tonight.'

Charlotte sipped at the cup and the warmth flowed through her body. She slipped away into sleep.

It was dark when she woke, there were candles giving light, her belly was on fire and the blankets were soaked.

12

She was cold again. She moved her legs and a foul smell came up from under the sodden bedclothes.

Angel Alexandra was at her side, 'You've got the fever dear, I can smell it.'

'What's that?'

'It often happens, but don't worry, it's never so bad with street births like yours. The doctors call it childbed fever, but you've got it quickly.'

Alexandra seemed a fount of all knowledge. 'I suppose you've had a lot of experience.' Charlotte was feeling very hot and her face was covered in beads of sweat. She turned in the bed to face her new friend, but let out a piercing yell. The movement had caused an excruciating stab of pain low in her belly.

There was a faint sound of a bell in the distance. A nurse scurried down to a bed in the corner and checked under the blanket, which had been drawn over the head of a nameless body.

'She's dead. The student doctors said she'd been a model patient, came in at just the right time three days ago, had a lovely little boy. They examined her a lot but she got the fever.'

The bell rang again, nearer.

'It's the priest and his sidekick, they come a long way to the dead.' In fact the gloomy procession had to pass through five wards to reach the first maternity division.

'I knew she was going when she thanked that lovely boy Prince Franz Joseph for coming to see her on his beautiful white horse and giving her an orchid.'

'Dreaming, was she?'

'Delirious, half way into the next world.'

The tuneless bell was loud now accompanied by heavy footsteps, and the well-nourished rosy-cheeked priest with a long purple nose hove into sight through the door. He was dressed in a black robe that barely concealed his enormous belly. He carried a book and a candle.

Behind this rotund pillar of the church a skeleton covered in skin, topped by a shock of white hair, trudged dutifully. He seemed to be bent double by the weight of the huge brass bell swinging from his right hand. The accompanying smell was of wine and rotting cabbages.

This doleful convoy was completed by a thickset man in a butcher's apron pushing a wheelbarrow.

'The last one's the mortuary attendant,' whispered Alexandra.

The comic trio passed without a glance to the living and proceeded to the dead woman's bed. There, the leader slurred a few well-chosen words, which would ensure that the departed soul had safe journey to its appointed destination.

With that completed, the corpse was lifted by the arms and legs and slung on to the barrow. The mournful group retreated from the ward under the sullen gaze of its remaining occupants.

'More meat for the mortuary.'

'Poor love, and with a good husband.'

'Who's next?'

Charlotte's head ached, her body felt on fire, her bed smelt awful, she wanted to vomit, movement gave her hell in her belly and all her joints had knives stuck in them. She was desperately thirsty.

Alexandra screamed in the next bed. 'Aagh! That wasn't a labour pain it was different, worse and longer. I know. My little Franz gave no trouble like this, there's got to be something wrong.' Gloom and doom descended on their corner of the room. Charlotte farted; she couldn't tell if she had soiled her bed even more.

14

4

The Interview Committee

Irma Valerie had changed into a clean, pressed but also black long cotton dress with a crimped frilly collar. This was the special dress that she wore for the great Professor Klein, whom she secretly adored and for these appointment interviews, which gave her sadistic pleasure.

She adjusted the date on the calendar on the boardroom wall. 21 June 1845, the large ornamental figures in the beautiful carved ebony frame declared to the high-ceilinged, chestnut wood-panelled room.

Placing the high-backed oak chair in the centre of the five for the appointments committee she gazed down at the seat. This is where the top man would sit along one side of the long polished table. This is where the director's bum would rest, supporting his considerable bulk. She was confused about the magnetism that drew her to him and stirred uncontrollable excitement between her thighs. It certainly was not the elephantine body topped by a bald round head or the podgy hands. But in that unlikely physique there lurked raw power.

The power over his women patients, the power to make or break the careers of young doctors and the power derived from his close contact with the great and good of Viennese society.

She suddenly turned and strode round to the other side

15

of the table to place the single uncushioned chair opposite the comfortable seats of the committee members.

There were five applicants for the post of aspirant lecturer to the first maternity clinic of the Vienna General Hospital. She knew only one of them: Franz Breit, a handsome self-assured young man. Too young, she thought. Of the others one was a foreigner, prematurely balding, with a bushy moustache. Ignaz Semmelweis was not her 'cup of tea', shy, serious and unglamorous.

She did not know the remaining three men but she had seen them on ward rounds; one of them had ludicrously taken it upon himself to carry a stool around for the professor to sit on at the bedside.

Irma knew that all five of the short-listed young doctors were capable of doing the job. She also knew that was not the only reason they had been summoned for interview.

Their presence boosted the egos of the committee, especially Klein's. It made the department's reputation as a centre of excellence more credible, and this was how things had always been done and there was no good reason to change. Of course no one admitted these things or really cared how these interviews could make or break the career of a young doctor. Instead when the subject was discussed at medical council the conclusion had always been, if they can't stand the heat they should get out of the kitchen.

The other members of the committee were the brilliant Joseph Skoda, expert at tapping the chest with his finger and favourite to be the next professor of medicine, although he was only thirty-nine years old.

Ferdinand Von Hebra was a skin doctor, whose researches into the scratching disease were becoming famous.

Then there was Rudolph Von Welden, a general physician given to administration and intrigue. He represented the grand office of the rector of the university. He was also rumoured to be a close friend and confidant of the foreign minister, Metternich.

Finally there was the external assessor, allegedly to see fair play and ensure that the best candidate was appointed. In fact this member of the panel had no influence, and his presence was merely a gesture to the liberal purists in the university. The dubious honour of occupying this final position on the committee fell today to dear old Professor Anton Schroeder; he was nearly ninety years old, partially blind, totally deaf and ga ga. An excellent choice for the purpose.

In his day Anton had been a kindly and conscientious tutor of pharmacology and therapeutics. He was fondly remembered by generations of doctors who had been coached by him, some of whom would probably never have passed their final examinations had it not been for his efforts. A sad aftermath of a dedicated career.

Irma Valerie was not aware that in ten days it would be the twenty-seventh birthday of Ignaz Fillipe Semmelweis. He had been born in Budapest, the fifth of the ten children of József and Terezia. She also did not know that currently he worked in the surgical and obstetric clinic, which he had done since graduating as a doctor the previous year.

However, Irma Valerie did know of the tremendous prestige of the Vienna General Hospital, which attracted doctors from the whole of the Austro-Hungarian Empire.

In 1844 Ignaz had decided to dedicate his life to obstetrics.

5

Transverse Lie

Charlotte seemed to have drunk buckets of water and still she was thirsty. However, she felt a little better. It was three hours since she had felt the pain in her belly and if anything it didn't hurt so much. But there was stickiness between her thighs and an awful smell coming from under her sweat-sodden blanket.

That nice young bald doctor with the bushy moustache had been to see her, put a hand on her forehead, then gently on her tummy, and even that had hurt terribly.

He had tried to reassure her. 'Charlotte,' he had said, 'you have childbed fever, but I think it is only mild. It seems to be less severe in you poor girls who have given birth in the street. Please drink lots of water and Nurse Anna will put a little sugar and salt in it to keep up your strength.'

'Yes, Dr Semmelweis.'

She hadn't seen this nurse before but she liked the friendly smile of the tall fair-haired woman, whom she guessed was in her thirties. Anna also seemed very respectful of the young man Charlotte now knew to be Dr Semmelweis. He never stopped working; he was the only doctor who was always around. She wondered when he slept.

They had now moved to Alexandra in the next bed. Her new-found friend was much quieter now but making under the window that looked on to the street was a chaise-longue upholstered in green velvet that matched the seats and backs of the six upright, armless chairs arranged around the room.

The wall opposite the entrance was completely covered with books, neatly shelved from floor to ceiling. As they came further into the room Charlotte turned to see the wall behind her held many pictures, mostly family portraits, including one of the late Alexandra, smiling and beautiful in happier days.

The other wall was almost filled by another set of double wooden doors containing frosted glass with a clear pattern of vines, through which a dining-room table could be glimpsed.

Charlotte took all this in with her quick, agile mind. She was also amazed how the children had greeted her and camouflaged their undoubted grief. She guessed (correctly) that Edith had conducted careful and kindly rehearsals.

'Let us be seated,' Rudolf indicated a high-backed chair, his guest sat. Alexandra started to howl and Georgina speedily returned her to her mother.

The little children perched on the chaise-longue, Rudolf sat opposite Charlotte and Edith remained standing.

'She's hungry, where can I—? Edith, please.'

Mother, baby and the house angel left the room. When they returned Kate was being hugged by her father and tears gently wiped away.

He broke the ice. 'I trust Alexandra has had a good supper.'

'Oh, yes, and I feel much more comfortable.' She smiled at everybody.

'Edith will show you your room. It will be your sanctuary. No one will come in unless you invite them.'

Once more the two left the room, climbed the stairs

to the first floor and Edith opened the door to one of the three rooms and ushered Charlotte in.

It was lovely; a small sash window still admitted a shaft of light from the sun as it moved round to the west. It looked down on to the quiet street. The walls were papered in pink and green stripes.

There was a neatly-made bed, on one side a cot and on the other a side table with paper and ink and a new pen lying on it. Under the windowsill was a chest of drawers with a small vase containing blue forget-me-nots with their yellow centres.

Charlotte laid Alexandra in her cot, tucked her in and said to Edith, 'I feel that I am in a dream.'

'Mr Rudolf is a kind, lovely man and it breaks my heart to see him grieve. They were such a happy couple and just as in love as the day they met twelve years ago. I have been with him in this house for fifteen years. Please bring joy back here.'

They left and went down the stairs and found Rudolf sitting alone. 'Come and sit with me and Edith will bring some refreshment.'

When they were alone: 'I now have two men to whom I have neither words nor means to show my gratitude.' At last tears poured down Charlotte's cheeks.

As she sobbed uncontrollably Rudolf stood up and gently laid a hand on top of her head, brushing it lightly down her long dark-brown hair. 'What did Dr Semmelweis say to you?'

Regaining her composure as best she could: 'I'm sorry for the tears. He said I should become a midwife, but I have little reading and less writing.'

'The tears need no apology; many have been shed in this house over the last days. Would you like to do it?'

'Yes, but I know it's not possible.'

'It is. Anyone who made the journey to the hospital

44

like you did can achieve the impossible. I will teach you, Edith will teach you and so will others. We will prepare you for the midwife school.'

11

Kolletschka's Counsel

As a foreign postgraduate Semmelweis' duties were essentially the same as those of the lecturer, the appointment he had failed to achieve. The young fair-haired, slightly balding Hungarian doctor with bright blue-grey eyes used the disappointment to fuel his energetic approach to work. But always dominating his thoughts were the ravages of puerperal fever.

Following his early morning study in the pathology institute, usually examining a victim of puerperal fever, he was beginning to notice some consistencies among the unfortunate women. There was frequently thick, foul-smelling fluid both in and around the still enlarged uterus. When he was finished the odour clung to his hands and he found that this could be partly alleviated by vigorously washing his hands in warm water, using a stiff bristle brush. Although the result looked clean the unpleasant smell lingered.

One early morning in August 1845 Leopold Kolletschka passed by this lonely spectacle sloshing water over the wooden floor of the pathology institute.

'There are lakes and the Danube for swimming, Ignaz.'

'Leo! Good morning. Haven't you noticed how the PM room smell clings to your hands?'

Kolletschka had been professor of forensic medicine for the past two years. A protégé of Karl Rokitanski, head of soft, rapid, moaning sounds. Dr Semmelweis was gently examining her swollen belly, a deepening frown appearing on his face. 'How long has she been in labour?'

'Nearly eighteen hours, doctor.' Anna was consulting a ledger she carried.

'I think it's a transverse lie and the womb is in spasm.'

Anna's free hand flew to her mouth in a gesture of horror. 'Are you sure?'

'I can feel the head out on the right; no wonder she is making no progress.'

Charlotte could only guess what 'transverse lie' meant. She knew that the baby's head usually came out first. If the baby was lying sideways in the birth passage it couldn't possibly get out. She was absolutely right.

'Can you turn it?' Anna asked Semmelweis.

'I'll have to try, otherwise she'll rupture her uterus.' He was speaking of the ghastly result of the baby being in such a position that delivery through the cervix and vagina cannot possibly take place.

In these circumstances of what is called mal-presentation the powerful contractions of the uterine muscles against an immovable obstruction cause it to rupture. From the torn muscle the patient bleeds to death.

'Nurse Anna, would you kindly fetch the tincture of laudanum and give the patient five drops.'

'Alexandra, we have a problem with the position of your baby in your womb.' The kindly voice continued. 'I am going to turn the head into the correct place.'

Alexandra nodded feebly that she understood, but she was too exhausted to reply or ask any questions.

The laudanum arrived and was given to the patient from a small goblet. She was too weak to lift her head from the pillow while she swallowed the small draught. It was hoped that this would temporarily relax the muscle of the uterus.

The kindly obstetrician was washing his hands meticulously in a bowl on a mobile three-legged stand. A strong but clean fresh smell came from the cloudy fluid. He shook drips from his fingers and reached for the clean white towel tucked neatly between the bowl and its supporting frame.

Charlotte watched, impressed and fascinated. A piercing, prolonged, agonised scream came from Alexandra. All heads – doctors, nurses, cleaners and patients – turned, in alarm, in her direction.

Her anguished face was white, sweat poured from her, hands clutched her swollen belly and her knees were drawn up. Breathing came in short shallow gasps and she vomited.

Ignaz Semmelweis knew he was too late; Alexandra's uterus had ruptured and was bleeding profusely into her peritoneal cavity. She was dying.

He gently laid a hand on her forehead as his other hand held one of hers. The pained expression on his face told of his helplessness.

'Please help me,' came faintly from Alexandra's lips. It was the last thing she said. The hugely dilated uterine arteries, which were this size to nurture her pregnancy, pumped out blood that could not be returned to her heart.

In less than five minutes she was dead. Tears cascaded down Charlotte's face, a seemingly endless, silent flood. She felt disconsolate, desolate and devastated; although known to her for only a few hours she had felt her to be her one true friend.

Fleetingly she had a sense of injustice because she felt physically better. No more pain, no shivering, no sweating and the smelly discharge between her legs was less.

Semmelweis and the nurse moved to the far end of the ward near the door, where two women were groaning, shaking and sweating. Charlotte again heard those two words – childbed fever.

She also heard that bloody bell in the distance gradually drawing nearer, heralding the ghoulish approach of the corpulent, wine-sodden man of god and his emaciated, bent, elderly retainer.

6

Pointless Charade

Ignaz wearily pressed open the heavy wooden door to the small waiting room outside the larger, grander boardroom.

He still wore the same bluish-grey frock coat, matching trousers and waistcoat he had been wearing on the ward. His shirt was white with a high stiff collar and a black, square-cut large bow tie.

It was his only suit and unlike his peers and seniors he regretted it. Theirs was almost a badge of office, worn proudly by many of them, that consisted of blood, urine and pus stains. Indeed, some of them even carried putrefying organs from the post-mortem room in their pockets. The foul smell didn't seem to bother them; Ignaz often wondered what it did to their sex lives.

The other four candidates were already there. Franz Breit sat in the only comfortable chair, arms folded, legs crossed and oozing a self-assured smugness. Rumour had it that he was rich, hunted and dined with the nobility and was invited to grand balls in the palaces of Vienna. Right up Klein's street, Ignaz reasoned glumly. He nodded at Breit, the friendliest gesture he could manage, and introduced himself formally to the other three. They were all Austrians, two from Vienna and the other from Salzburg.

He had met them briefly from their visits on Klein's

ward round. He discovered them to be a year younger than himself and correspondingly earlier in their careers. They all told Ignaz that they were surprised to be short-listed for such a prestigious appointment in the world of obstetrics, which was widely accepted in south-east Europe to lead to a glittering and lucrative career.

As usual they would be interviewed in alphabetical order, which meant that Semmelweis would be the last to face the committee. He groaned inwardly; it was always a disadvantage. The longer he waited the more nervous he became. He also suspected that sometimes members of such interviewing panels became bored towards the end and the fine wine, large prostates and prospect of an excellent dinner made them impatient.

Irma Valerie appeared at the door and announced that the committee to appoint an aspirant lecturer to the first maternity clinic of the Vienna General Hospital was now in session. 'Dr Breit, please.' The cocksure young man swaggered past the lady in black who made a ridiculous little curtsy as he brushed against her.

The door closed after them both and the atmosphere in the little ante-room lightened considerably.

'Arrogant little shit,' murmured one young man. The others smiled in agreement.

Semmelweis, fair-minded as ever, reflected that although he disliked Franz Breit for his influence and social connections with the nobility he had to admit that he was a good obstetrician, well read and with good hands. However, he did give the impression to the patients that they belonged with the squashed cockroaches on the sole of his shoe.

Apart from the single remark as Breit's back disappeared they sat there in silence, one or other of them taking a particularly deep breath from time to time.

Twenty minutes later Breit came back in. The broad

smirk on his face announced, 'You poor buggers, they're going to give it to me, I was brilliant, I've got it all buttoned up.' He said nothing but the message was clear. Irma Valerie returned, smiled broadly at Breit and then leered at the others. Her message, too, was unmistakable. She was really enjoying herself.

One by one the other three nervous young men went in to be interviewed. They remained behind the closed door for shorter and shorter periods, the last being afforded only five minutes.

As he was ushered back out Professor Anton's raised voice could be heard, 'I wanted to ask him about pain relief in labour.' As the door closed Klein's rasping riposte could just be heard, 'Go back to sleep, you silly old fool!'

At last it was the turn of Semmelweis and he followed the exuberant Irma Valerie into the chestnut-panelled room. He did not notice the massive paintings of hunting scenes nor the row of portraits on the opposite wall. His gaze was concentrated on the five men behind the table.

Irma Valerie gave an imperious wave towards the hard chair opposite the committee before taking her place standing behind Klein.

Semmelweis sat down and softly bade the assembly, 'Good afternoon, gentlemen.'

'Good afternoon,' boomed Klein. He deliberately withheld the name of the man sitting opposite him. This was unbelievably rude and offensive and almost certainly reflected his contempt for a Hungarian daring to come to civilised Vienna and apply for such an exalted post.

'You know Dr Von Hebra and Dr Skoda, I presume. They are nearly as famous as me.' He roared with laughter at this attempted joke in poor taste and inappropriate circumstances.

'I do, sir,' Ignaz replied unsmilingly.

'My esteemed colleague Dr Von Welden represents the

rector of the University of Vienna and Professor Anton Schroeder is here to see fair play.'

'Thank you,' Semmelweis glanced over at the aged academic whose bewhiskered chin had sunk on to his chest, eyes closed and gently snoring. Klein made no attempt to rouse him. 'I see from your *curriculum vitae* that you have recently qualified as doctor of medicine.'

'Yes, sir, from the University of Pest on April twenty-first last year.'

'You plan a career in obstetrics?' The question was hurried, the tone bored and the implication of no reply preferred.

'I am shortly sitting for my master of obstetrics diploma and will know the result on first of August next.'

Klein nodded; he was anxious to get this over. Von Welden had promised to introduce him to an excellent moselle wine and a voluptuous Italian soprano after the meeting. 'Any questions, gentlemen?'

'You a hunting man? I hear there are fine stags in Hungary.' Von Welden's irrelevant enquiry was barbed.

'I wouldn't know about that.'

'What would you know about?'

Ignaz tried to maintain his composure in front of this stupid arrogant fool. 'I am greatly interested by the paper read to the Association of Physicians by Oliver Wendell Holmes in Boston last October.'

'And what may that be about?' The tone was impatient and condescending.

'The possible contagiousness of puerperal fever.' Klein's double chin wobbled with the guffaw that Semmelweis' statement produced. 'Ridiculous rubbish, eh, Dr Von Welden?'

'Complete nonsense,' agreed the arrogant, arse-licking administrator. His sly smile was more of a smirk. No such mirth was forthcoming from Von Hebra or Skoda. Anton snored.

'I would like to hear more,' Josef Skoda said quietly.

'There's no time,' snapped Klein rudely. 'The interview is over. We will deliberate tomorrow.'

Semmelweis sensed that the interview had gone badly; he rose and, with a slight formal bow, left. Anton snored on.

7

A Friend Indeed

Charlotte was feeling much better in her body. The fever had gone, the foul discharge was much less and the smell was greatly reduced but still offensive. She was hungry. But she was still deeply depressed by the death of Alexandra.

Her breasts were swollen and uncomfortable and she guessed that they were filling up with milk. She had not seen her baby daughter since the midwife who had cut the cord had taken her just after she arrived. She now had a powerful desire to see and hold her little girl.

As if by nature's immaculate timing, Nurse Anna appeared at the doorway carrying a bundle wrapped in a green woollen towel. It was howling.

The tall elegant nurse walked purposefully towards Charlotte and all the eyes of the other patients followed her progress.

'Your daughter's hungry.' She smiled warmly as she gently handed the precious parcel to its mother.

Charlie took the baby hesitantly and for the first time saw her clean, dry and in daylight. Huge tears rolled silently down both cheeks as she gazed into the big blue eyes of the ravenous baby.

'I know I'm your mother but you really are beautiful.' The tears continued unabated.

27

'Now you give her her lunch and then I'll give you yours,' laughed Anna.

One first toe was peeping out from under the blanket and tied to it with a pink ribbon was a white label with 'Charlie's Angel 19 June 1845' written in exquisite copperplate.

She exposed her breast and instantly the little mouth found its way to the nipple. The howling stopped and there was peace and contentment in mother and child.

'You'll have to give her a name,' her neighbour kindly advised.

Charlotte's lunch arrived: warm soup with a little cabbage and even less beef and a large brown bread roll. She started to eat and found herself really enjoying the meagre fare.

While chewing on her crusty victuals she seriously considered her neighbour's advice. The emotions of the last three days crowded in on her but the death of Alexandra dominated her thoughts.

'I shall call her Alexandra, she announced. Alexandra Weiss.'

There was spontaneous and loud applause from all the ladies in the vast room. Even those with the fever and near to death managed to clap their hands as they all became united in their approval and suffering.

Charlotte's father, Charles Weiss, had been a much respected clock maker in Vienna. However, his skills with pendulums and cog wheels had not been matched by his abysmal bookkeeping. Many bills went unpaid and his clientèle, particularly the rich and powerful, took advantage of him.

Two months before Charlotte was born, Charles Weiss was killed by four great horses that were pulling an opulent coach along a Vienna street being terrified by a bolt of lightning and running amok. He left a small business in

used on the opposite side by the candidates. This is where she was going to sit.

At one end was a place marked with a card bearing the name Prof. Anton Schroeder. 'Well out of the way where the old fool can rest in the arms of Morpheus and not interfere with the wishes of my dear Johann,' she said out loud to the empty room.

She had placed Von Welden at the other end and knew that he would agree with whatever Klein wanted. He had already sold his soul to the devil. She had been present when he had certified that two anarchists that Metternich had had murdered had died of natural causes.

Opposite her idol she placed Skoda and Von Hebra. For this particular exercise she regarded them as dangerous. She had no idea why they sat on this committee.

Joseph Skoda was head of the department of chest diseases. His boyish good looks gainsaid his thirty-nine years and brilliant mind. Six years earlier he had introduced the prototype of the first stethoscope, which was already having a huge impact on diagnosis around the world.

Ferdinand Von Hebra was technically assistant to the chest physician but in charge of the department of infectious skin diseases. He was investigating the 'scratching' ailment and about to demonstrate that it was caused by a tiny burrowing mite one-third of a millimetre long – scabies.

She had placed quill pens and ink, paper, glasses and carafes of water at each place. In the carafe of her adored professor she had added a generous portion of Russian vodka, which she knew he required to settle the stomach after a difficult night working on behalf of his department among the benevolent high society of Vienna.

Finding everything pleasing to her eagle eyes she marched to the door and opened it with a flourish. To her amazement Anton Schroeder was slumped against the wall outside and it was only a quarter to nine. 'Can't sleep long at night these days,' he mumbled and lurched towards his allotted place.

'That's because you sleep all day,' said Irma under her breath.

Skoda and Von Hebra arrived at nine o'clock precisely, nodded a cheerful 'Good Morning' to an already snoring Anton and took their places at the table.

Von Welden ambled in shortly afterwards, ignored everyone present, lit a cigar and farted. He knew he was disliked and distrusted by the clinicians at the cutting edge of patient care and research. He did not bother to cultivate a harmonious relationship with his colleagues; instead he relied on his connections in high places to secure his position.

The assembled four doctors with Irma Valerie standing by Klein's chair sat and waited and waited.

Klein lumbered in twenty-one minutes late, offered no apology to his colleagues, and mumbled something about a difficult birth he had been called to attend at the Russian Embassy.

Skoda politely enquired if the difficulty involved delivering the cork from the bottle. Klein glowered as Irma Valerie took his arm and guided him to his chair. Even she had to admit to herself that her beloved chief was suffering from a monumental hangover.

He was clearly not in the mood for a long meeting, 'We interviewed five candidates for the post of aspirant lecturer in obstetrics yesterday. There is no doubt in my mind that the best man for the appointment is Dr Franz Breit.' He held up his hand to silence any interruption from the opposite side of the table.

'Dr Breit is an outstanding obstetrician, has followed my methods exactly and is well connected.'

'I agree entirely,' Von Welden started to rise from his seat. He already had his advisory fee in mind and the

34

lunch it would fund with Sophie, the buxom daughter of an army captain. She willingly satisfied his penchant for slurping oysters from her belly button. She had also promised other excitements.

'We have not discussed the other candidates,' Von Hebra's tone was belligerent. Von Welden sat back in his chair with a muttered, 'There's no need.'

Joseph Skoda saw the problem. The panel had been rigged, and there was no intention of appointing the doctor who had the greatest merit. He tried to rescue the situation, 'I agree that there is little to choose between the three other Austrians. However, the Hungarian, Ignaz Semmelweis, has a passion and intensity about him. He is concerned about the large number of deaths from childbed fever in previously healthy mothers. He is studying factors here in Vienna and also the work in this field outside Austria, particularly the paper of Oliver Wendell Holmes at Harvard University. I feel he should be encouraged to continue his work in this higher post.'

'Had a chat with the little bald foreigner, eh?' sneered Klein. 'Highly improper.'

The professor's face turned purple and his neck veins were prominent as he failed to suppress his anger. 'We'll put it to the vote.'

Irma Valerie stood up. 'A show of hands, please, gentlemen.' She loved this bit. 'Dr Franz Breit.' Klein and Von Welden instantly raised an arm. Irma Valerie viciously kicked the snoring Anton's right ankle, both arms shot up in the air. 'No further vote required,' she announced. 'I will inform Dr Breit of his success and the others of their failure.'

She smiled at Johann Klein, he nodded, she turned and left the room with a clatter of heels. She just caught Von Hebra's, 'Outrageous,' faintly borne on her slipstream.

9

Aftermath

Lajos Markusovszky sat in a high-backed chair with wooden arms and upholstered in green and white striped silk, which was a little threadbare.

He was reading an ancient copy of *The Whole Course of Surgery* by Peter Lowe, having seen it on a street-market bookstall. It had been published in London in 1597 although the author worked in Paris and was surgeon to the King of France.

He had been attracted to both the preface addressed to 'the friendly reader' and a set of amazing drawings at the end, including a picture of an operation for cleft lip. The instruments shown were similar to those available in Vienna over two hundred years later.

He was a fine looking man with a full beard and moustache neatly trimmed and sported the fashionable bow tie. He was thirty years old, a lecturer in the surgical department and shared a small apartment with Semmelweis near the Vienna General.

They were close friends, held similar opinions and were equally devoted to the welfare of patients. He was so startled by a loud knocking on the front door that he dropped his book to the floor.

He got up, took the few short paces on the polished boards to the front door which opened directly into the living room. He lifted the simple latch and pulled.

'I am so sorry, Lajos, I came back here to smarten up before the interview and left the key on my bed.' Semmelweis' face betrayed his dejection.

'Come in, Ignaz, tell me all about it.'

The story unfolded in as much of the detail as was known to Semmelweis. His friend listened in silence. At last he related how Irma Valerie had waltzed into the waiting room, her sallow face showing an unusual tinge of red on the cheeks, and she was a little breathless. Her voice was less strident and unusually husky but nevertheless forceful. Ignaz made no attempt to imitate but quoted; 'Gentlemen, the appointments committee chaired by the great Professor Klein has deliberated and the following have been unsuccessful in their applications for the post of lecturer in obstetrics.'

She had then read out the names including that of Semmelweis, and could not control a sneering tone when mispronouncing the Hungarian's name.

The clearly excited Irma Valerie then turned to Franz Breit, gave a beaming smile revealing yellowing teeth and announced, 'You, Dr Breit, are the new aspirant lecturer to the first maternity clinic of the Vienna General Hospital. Your duties will be performed under the director, the much celebrated Professor Johann Klein, who has been the dazzling star of the obstetrics department for the past twenty-three years.'

She strode over to Breit, held out her hand, which he delicately held and kissed. No firm handshake here. Someone in the room could not suppress his giggle. She released her hand, turned, glowered at the suspected offender and swept out of the room like the queen she certainly was not.

When Semmelweis had finished, he sat back in his chair and sighed, '*C'est la vie.*'

Markusovsky leaned forward in his chair and their eyes met. 'Ignaz, my friend, you have suffered a great injustice. I know your knowledge, skill, gentleness and great industry made you by far the best candidate for the job.'

He paused for a moment and was pleased to see his friend's face brighten. 'God only knows what it is between that woman and Klein. Your description of her suggested she was getting some sexual gratification from the whole thing.'

'Odd, isn't it?' Semmelweis' natural innocence showed.

'Very odd indeed. That great lump only dazzles at Metternich's dinner table with his obscene witticisms at the expense of his patients. Sure he's celebrated, for presiding over the increase in puerperal fever in his department from 1 per cent in 1822 to 7 per cent in 1823. And it has remained high. The man's a bad joke!'

Semmelweis' brain filed the information and remembered that 1822 was the date routine post-mortems were introduced on obstetric fatalities.

'You know, Ignaz, as well as I, that the only way to bounce back from your disappointment is to get down to work.' He paused. 'Now.'

His friend was right. Ignaz still functioned as aspirant externist in the first obstetric clinic, which he had done since graduating as a doctor in 1844.

During this time he had risen at four-thirty each morning to perform post-mortems, mainly on patients who had died of puerperal fever. He did this, taking careful notes for two hours before moving on to his main work with the women in labour, where he attended to their difficulties.

He had, even at that time, made use of a chlorine hand wash between the two activities. In order to do this work in the department of pathological anatomy he had obtained permission from its head, Professor Karl Rokitanski, who had shown him kindness and given encouragement.

He had also during that time in pathology met Professor Jakob Kolletschka who had been made professor of forensic medicine a year previously. They became good friends despite a fifteen-year age difference.

Lajos and Ignaz set off for the hospital although they were going to make a brief stop at one of Vienna's famous coffee shops. There was a spring in their step, Ignaz' head was up and his shoulders were well braced back. The world seemed a better place and there was much to be done.

10

Going Home

Charlotte was fully dressed; her clothes had been washed and ironed by some of her fellow patients. Even her purple coat had been lovingly tended and looked remarkably smart. A dexterous but anonymous seamstress had worked on the loose threads and bare areas with wonderful success.

She sat on a wooden chair in the middle of the vast maternity ward. Baby Alexandra was in her arms, quiet, having been breastfed five minutes earlier. Her mother now felt well, her lochia was very slight and she had a healthy appetite both for nourishment and for life. She was, however, acutely aware of the sounds and smells of impending tragedy that surrounded her. She eagerly awaited the arrival of Rudolf Orlov.

The first man to enter through the high oak door was Dr Semmelweis accompanied by the midwife Sofia who had also been kind to Charlotte.

Ignaz saw her ready for departure. His kind and gentle nature took him straight to her. 'You have a beautiful baby and she has a courageous mother.'

'Thank you, Dr Semmelweis.'

'I wish you and your child every good fortune.' He gave a little bow.

'Sir,' said Charlotte, touching the cuff of his coat sleeve,

'I have not the words to show my gratitude. I believe you saved my life and I can give you nothing.'

'Young lady, it was my duty.' At that moment Rudolf appeared in the doorway. As Semmelweis turned to leave he said, 'Give thought to becoming a midwife.'

'But I can barely read and—' he was gone and Rudolf was approaching, his face no longer sad, but still serious. He managed a faint smile.

'Come little mother and Alexandra, it's time to go home.' The tone was warm, although Charlotte was not so sure about the 'little'; she was five feet ten inches tall.

Rudolf's face registered surprise when she stood up. He took her arm and they walked from the ward to murmured, 'Bye, dears', 'Good luck' and one 'Try not to come back.'

They passed along the dark corridors of the vast building and emerged into the bright sunshine of the Vienna summer, where a one-horse open coach and driver was waiting for them.

Their horse trotted briskly, taking them past awninged shops, street traders with stalls of flowers, books and peddlers of all manner of items, including fortune-telling cards.

As the coach took them east the tall spire and unique zigzag pattern roof of St Stephen's Cathedral could be seen towering above the centre of the city.

Long before they reached the hub of Vienna the coachman steered them left into a narrow street with tall houses freshly painted and well maintained.

They gently came to a halt outside number ten, a three-storey green and white terraced house.

There had been no words during the journey, Charlotte marvelling at the sights and sounds of the bustling city. Her attention was also directed at the safety of the baby in her arms as they bounced over the cobbled streets.

41

Rudolf appeared content with the absence of conversation. The dark-green front door opened and at the top of the six stone steps leading up to it stood a plump, short, rosy-cheeked lady in a long grey dress and starched white apron.

She greeted the arrivals with a broad smile and three little faces were peeping at them inquisitively around her voluminous skirts.

Rudolf stepped down into the street and stretched out both hands, which Charlotte took to steady herself while holding Alexandra in the crook of her right arm, as she alighted on to the narrow pavement. They moved up towards the door.

'This is Edith, my house angel, and behind her my three little rascals, Georgina, Franz and Kate. I believe they are still the apples of their mother's eye.'

The three children stepped forward around Edith's dress as she gave a heartfelt, 'Welcome my dears, all of you.'

Georgina, a beautiful ten-year-old with deep blue eyes, curly long blonde hair, wearing a long powder-blue dress, curtsied. 'Hello, Charlotte. May I hold Alexandra?'

The new mother, feeling safe, placed her baby in the girl's already cradled arms. 'Hello Georgina.'

Franz was aged seven with light brown hair, blue eyes and sporting a brown tweed suit. He gave a formal little bow and extended his right hand, which was accepted. 'How do you do, Charlotte? I am very pleased to meet you.'

Kate, who was four, with black straight hair and the brown eyes of her father, managed her curtsy in a maroon velvet dress, then ran forward and hugged Charlotte around the knees. A loving hand ruffled her hair.

Edith ushered them into the dark narrow hallway and then through double wooden doors to the right into the drawing room. In the centre was a small round table;

the pathology department in Vienna and future rector of the university.

'It's a great problem, my friend. There are times when my wife won't let me in the house until I've scrubbed my hands and arms raw and sometimes bleeding.'

'Is there any way to protect your skin?'

'I always rub in oil on my hands and arms before work and wash with soap and water afterwards.'

'Does it work? Do you get the key to your own front door?'

Jakob Leopold Kolletschka gave a deep sigh. 'Not completely, but I have found that water that has chlorine gas bubbled through it helps to give a clean smell.'

Ignaz' keen young mind filed another little known piece of information away.

He finished washing his hands. 'Of course your work in forensic pathology gives you a wide variety of people who have died, sometimes in mysterious circumstances.'

'In terms of smell the worst are those that have been dragged out of the Danube. They are massively bloated and the gas that is released is truly foul at the first touch of the autopsy knife.' Kolletschka wrinkled his nose as he spoke.

Ignaz persisted, 'Do you think the release of these gases harm our patients?'

'It certainly harms our noses, but we don't see many people walking around with a gangrenous black proboscis about to fall off.'

'Yet all the top men talk about miasma or noxious vapours as the cause of puerperal fever, and they even blame the planet earth with talk of telluric influences.'

'I agree with you, young man. I too have listened to your boss, Klein, waffle on endlessly along those lines. He is a big man here in Vienna, people nod their heads in sage agreement without thought or —'

47

'Face the end of their careers,' interrupted Ignaz.

'Especially if they are young foreigners, as you learned to your cost in that interview last month. Tread carefully, the boat moves best when it is not rocked.'

'You know how much these dead mothers and babies affect me.'

'I do, and the babies born to these unfortunate women have collections of foul fluid in their peritoneal cavities, chest and brains like their mothers have exhibited.'

'How do I move the boat without rocking it?'

Kolletschka was silent for a few moments. 'We are in a period of great change. Science, not baseless theories, is the way forward. Collect facts and figures and analyse them. Speak respectfully at scientific meetings. You may have new ideas but don't be too ready to condemn the old ones.'

'I am grateful for your words.'

'Remember, people like Klein have been around a long time, they are powerful in the hospital and have powerful friends. They don't fall easily or gracefully.'

Ignaz left the post-mortem building deep in thought and headed for the first maternity clinic to prepare the presentation of the patients for the professor's ward round.

12

First Obstetric Clinic

At eight o'clock precisely on the morning of 28 August 1845 Ignaz Semmelweis pushed open the great oak door of the first obstetric clinic of the Vienna General Hospital. The sun was already shining through the windows high on the east wall, revealing the neat parallel rows of beds on each side of the vast room. The ward was unusually quiet although a buzz of female voices could be heard coming from one of the doors at the far end.

No other doctor was there. He was pleased to be the first to arrive; as a Hungarian he had to do that much more to keep pace with his Austrian colleagues.

He unassumingly passed between the rows of women, giving a warm friendly smile to those who looked his way. Outside the day was fine and fresh but inside the smell was there, unmistakable, putrefying – it was always there.

As he approached the far end of the lying-in room he saw the softly moaning devastation of puerperal fever. A trembling, scared, sweating grey-faced woman had flung the sheets off her in an attack of fevered delirium. She lay there naked and shuddering in a heap of linen stained with dark blood and putrid material.

The white part of her eyes was deep yellow and her gasping breath ceased completely shortly after Semmelweis stopped by her bed and took her limp hand in his.

The young man's spirits crashed and he felt the weight of the world on his shoulders.

'Don't take it so personally, Dr Semmelweis.' A short fair-haired nurse in her middle thirties emerged from the door of the staff office. 'She has been in great pain in the early hours and laudanum gave her peace. Childbed fever again.'

'Such a sad loss of a young woman; and the baby?

'Died three hours ago. Mother had been in labour for nineteen hours, Dr Breit eventually used the forceps yesterday morning when the head was low enough. Just after he returned from the post-mortem room. They were both fine after that. The fever started at ten yesterday evening, it was all over very fast.'

Nurse Violetta was new to Semmelweis and he liked the motherly feelings she displayed, but her words left him with a sense of incompleteness, something not done.

'I have sent for the mortuary attendant, there's nothing more we can do. I have the list of admissions during the night that are waiting for you to clerk.'

Semmelweis approached the first of his day's duties with muted enthusiasm as he followed Violetta to the first bed.

'Good morning. My name is Dr Semmelweis and I would like to ask you about yourself and examine you to assess progress.'

As he spoke he sat on a plain wooden chair and took a sheaf of papers from Violetta and placed them on the small table beside him where pen and ink were already present.

'My name is Teresa Kruger. I am twenty years old. This is my second baby, my first is thirteen months now, a lovely boy, and I have been having pains for five hours.'

The cheerful smile and twinkling blue eyes told him she knew the routine, but her blonde eyebrows shot up in surprise when he asked, 'Is your appetite good? Do you have any breathing problems or chest pains?'

She was not expecting the more general enquiries and was impressed by his thoroughness. She winced as a contraction gripped her but remained calm.

For her it was natural that he should then examine her. For him rinsing his hands in a nearby bowl of water on a wooden washstand also seemed natural.

However, what did not seem natural to him was the traditional method of both examining and performing procedures with the patients exposed on their backs with knees flexed and thighs separated, with the vagina fully exposed.

'Surely,' said Ignaz to Nurse Violetta, 'this position is not necessary merely to palpate the baby in the uterus.'

'But it is the standard routine, doctor.'

'I know, but a relaxed dignified patient would seem to me to reveal more to the palpating hand.'

'I can't allow the change, doctor. It's more than my job's worth.'

'I understand.' He completed both external and internal examinations gently without delay.

'Your cervix is nearly fully dilated and your baby will arrive soon.'

He gently patted the back of her hand before carefully writing all the history and examination details down on her case sheet, which he initialled 'I S, 08.30hrs, 28.08.45'.

He was then conducted to the next woman in labour by Violetta. She was attentive, helpful and slightly more respectful than when they had begun.

By this time the other junior doctors had appeared and began clerking the patients allocated to them, albeit with a little less history taking, a little less writing and a little more intrusive examination.

Ignaz clerked three more patients with the help of

51

Violetta. One of his quartet had a breast abscess that required draining.

The doctors gathered together and arranged the operations that were required.

Ignaz' patient was taken by Violetta into the small operating theatre adjacent to the nurses' office. Medical students were already in place on the raised semicircular observation benches. Their chattering partially ceased when the apprehensive patient was brought in and laid upon the wooden operating table.

Here was the essential difference from the second obstetrics clinic, where midwives were trained but did not have the hands-on activity of the students.

The patient was already sedated and Ignaz had the ignominy of assisting Breit with the procedure. The incision was swiftly made and thick green fluid gushed out under pressure. Although the brave young mother felt the pain of the scalpel she breathed out a sigh of relief when the tension and intense throbbing were released.

The next lady requiring surgical intervention had been seen by Dr Breit repeatedly over the past twenty hours until he left the hospital twelve hours ago. She had been in slow labour, her membranes had ruptured, the cervix was dilating, but shortly after he left the labour pains became less frequent. He had been surprised she had not delivered during the night.

She walked in with a nurse supporting her and was helped on to the table. The sheet on the table was unchanged but only a little of the discharge from the breast had left a dull green stain on the edge.

The woman was exhausted, it was her first baby and she had done all she could with the midwives shouting, 'Push!', to expel the head.

'I shall use forceps,' Breit announced to his audience. The nurses lifted her floppy legs and he applied the two parts of the instrument to the baby's head. He closed the handles and lifted the head clear of the vagina. '*Voilà!*' he waved the forceps above his head and paraded in front of the applauding students.

The important work to finish the delivery was being attended to by midwives, cutting the cord, reviving the baby and supervising the afterbirth.

Semmelweis murmured under his breath, 'Pompous and lucky.'

In fact, although this dramatic display looked easy, it was easy. Ignaz had also examined the patient at Breit's request, covering his reputation in case he made a fool of himself in public.

It was now necessary to select a woman with a childbirth condition that merited a focus for the professor to use to teach the students.

The case chosen was a woman with puerperal fever.

13

Vocation In View

The candle flickered in the late August breeze as it stole through a chink between the window and frame, warped by the severe Vienna winter.

Charlotte dipped her quill in the ink-well and for the third time in a clear and increasingly stylish hand wrote:

The stars move still, time runs, the clock will strike.
The devil will come and Faustus must be damned.

Edith had spent many hours coaching the handwriting, spelling and grammar. There had been many 'practice makes perfect's. Misspelt words had been repeatedly re-written and errors in grammar corrected, then recited out loud.

As a reward for progress Charlotte had been allowed to develop her own curlicues and flourishes on favoured letters, such as 'A' for Alexandra.

The baby seemed to sense that she was not the only project in her mother's life. She did demand her feeds but with a mellifluous gurgle that was easy on the eardrums and soon satisfied. The children, especially Georgina, delighted in attending to Alexandra's needs but did not deny Charlotte the essential cuddles.

Rudolf was responsible for the content of this crash

course. As he had handed the red leatherbound and gold-embossed copy of Christopher Marlowe's 1604 *Tragical History of Dr Faustus* he tenderly pressed her hands on to the cover.

'You cannot learn everything, but you can have a framework on which to build. The basics are reading, writing and training your memory.'

His tenderness and concern showed as he continued, 'Your reasoning, observation and humanity are also evolving in this period.' Pointing to the volume, 'I have marked a short passage for you to memorise and then write with the book closed.'

Charlotte was anxious to please but fatigue was beginning to numb her mind. She said nothing, sat down and opened the marked page.

'I know you are weary, it is the time nature seeks out our strengths. When you are done, sleep well and we will analyse the piece tomorrow.'

He had cautiously entered her room after knocking and now slipped out quietly.

She did exactly as he had requested and there followed deep, refreshing, satisfied sleep with Alexandra at her side.

Tutoring Charlotte and caring for Alexandra soon became part of the routine of the household. During the week Rudolf was at work at the office of the minister for the army and at the weekends there were visits to the parks and fairs of Vienna.

On Sunday after lunch the whole family, including the new mother and child, went to lay flowers at the grave of Alexandra. Little was said by husband or children but the grieving was clear and intense.

On the evening after Charlotte had learned that strange piece about Dr Faustus she was sitting opposite Rudolf by the fire with the children on their favoured chaise-longue under the window.

Progress that day had been good. She was thrilled when Edith having seen her writing practice had said, 'Young lady, you are becoming a woman of accomplishment.'

Looking across at Rudolf she felt the nagging doubt that had been there from the first moment in the hospital when he had invited her here. Why her? What did he want? Since her arrival in this lovely home she had never felt threatened, never at risk of any sort. She remained puzzled. 'Faustus wanted it all, wealth, success, fame, women, contentment and everlasting youth.' Rudolf's voice brought her back to reality in a flash. 'It was all possible, except the youth part, but he wanted it instantly, without work, without effort and without end.'

'And in the real world?'

'It just doesn't happen.' He raised his voice very slightly, 'but in Faustus' world there was the devil with only one appetite, the good doctor's soul.'

'What is its relevance for me?'

'You will achieve, you are succeeding and it shows.' He took a deep breath and carried on. 'The gifts you needed were opportunity, a roof over your head and sustenance.'

'I know.'

Rudolf gave an inkling of passion. "These are human rights, they should not be for sale, even for the highest price.'

As she listened intently a tear rolled down Charlotte's left cheek. She did not move.

'I have given you what I can and cannot say why. It has been a team effort. Edith has been the captain, my children have been included, as have both Alexandras. I think you are ready for midwifery school.'

For the second time in their relationship all Charlotte could manage was, 'Thank you.'

14

The Grand Round

Professor Johann Klein was appointed head of the obstetric clinic of the Vienna General Hospital in 1822. He was in his thirty-fifth year and had eagerly accepted the promotion from his post in Salzburg.

Vienna offered him the most prestigious midwifery position in the Austro-Hungarian Empire and put him on a par with his colleagues in Paris and Berlin. From here he would be able to dictate the curriculum of the training of midwives and doctors throughout his vast domain.

He had succeeded Professor Johann Lucas Boer, who had been a keen supporter of natural childbirth. He had promoted less interference, stopped purges and bloodletting. At the end of his tenure marked by reform the incidence of puerperal fever in the department was 1.25 per cent.

In his early years Klein had adhered to the role of professor holding a university departmental chair. This included teaching, research, administration and sitting on the advisory committees of appointments and policy.

Early in his elevated position he had diverted university funds to assign himself a personal assistant. The young Irma Valerie was at that time a tall elegant dark-haired young woman with a smooth olive complexion and dark brown eyes, which even his few friends said gave an impression of deviousness.

Klein had immediately become captivated by his young assistant. However, over the years he had allowed his infatuation to permit her to expand her influence over doctors, midwives, patients and every facet of his department.

He had lusted after her in the early days but he could never free his mind from the ever-present and overbearing presence of his wife, who claimed a distant connection with Queen Amalie of Saxony. He suspected her family had influenced his career. He dare not cross her. Whatever had or had not happened between the good professor and Irma Valerie she never wavered from her devoted and ruthless support of Klein.

In the world of medical science the new head of the department was a man of paradox. Shortly after his appointment he had introduced the practice of post-mortem examinations on all the patients who had died in the maternity department, but had apparently not noticed that at the end of the first year of this practice the mortality rate from puerperal fever had risen to 7.45 per cent.

In 1833 the maternity department was divided into first and second clinics by Klein. From 1839 he directed medical students be assigned to the first and pupil midwives to the second obstetrics clinics respectively.

The Grand Round was the academic highpoint of the obstetric department's week. Lecturers, junior doctors, midwives, pupil midwives and medical students all attended.

Anyone missing without good and previously notified reason was duly noted by Irma Valerie who would ensure as much as she could that it affected the absentee's career.

Wednesday was the day, ten o'clock the time and on this occasion, 15 September the date. All were present in the centre of the lying-in ward of the first obstetric clinic of the Vienna General Hospital. Among them Ignaz Fillipe Semmelweis.

The hushed whispers of the throng became silence as

the great door at the entrance to the huge room crashed open. The top man strode purposefully if a little unsteadily towards the group. Irma Valerie, clutching her black attendance book, made a ridiculous little curtsy.

'Well, gentlemen?' The omission of the women who far outnumbered the men in the address was noticed by Ignaz but apparently by nobody else. 'What have you for me today?' boomed a beaming Klein.

'Sir,' said Franz Breit, 'the case I would like to present to you is one of puerperal fever.' He turned and indicated with an almost unnoticeable gesture a pale, sweating, shivering woman in a nearby bed. The group broke open the circle surrounding the chief and allowed him to view the subject of the seminar. Harsh breathing, soft moaning and the unmistakable foul odour came from her.

'A subject I understand perfectly,' Klein wrinkled his bulbous nose. 'Who are the presenters?'

'Mr Pfeiffer will introduce the history, Mr Biritz the physical examination and Mr Schweizer the differential diagnosis.'

The format was routine. The students introduced the subject and the professor led the discussion.

'Excellent,' beamed the professor.

"This lady is Mrs Annelie Bormann. She is twenty-three years old and eighteen hours ago she was delivered of her second child. She had been in labour five hours. The placenta was expelled after a further thirty-five minutes. The baby appeared healthy but developed acute respiratory failure after fifty-five minutes and died.'

Ignaz admired the student's sensitive and well-rehearsed introduction and looked forward to the Hungarian student Biritz's description of the physical findings.

However, Klein was irritated. 'Come on, come, on this is becoming a snail race.' His fingers drummed on the lapels of his waistcoat.

Biritz began. 'Examination at nine this morning showed a distressed young lady with fever, pain and having rapid shallow respiration. In the abdomen—'

'More expeditious, Magyar.' The tone was insulting. 'We know all that, get to the meat of the matter.' Klein was impatient to get to his starring role.

The young Hungarian student could not hide his crestfallen feelings but continued. 'Movement with respiration was reduced, palpation with my hand showed great tenderness, especially in the lower part.'

'And on vaginal examination, young man?'

'I did not do it.'

'You did not do it, you did not do it.' As the professor repeated himself his voice became stridently louder and spittle appeared at the corners of his mouth. 'We are obstetricians, not swooning swains. Why?'

'There was no midwife available,' the persecuted young man's voice fell away in the last two words.

'No midwife available.' The great Johann Klein seemed unable to produce words of his own. An uneasy shuffling of feet was the only sound in the pregnant pause.

He advanced on the terrified dying young woman, roughly spread her legs and plunged two fingers into the discharging inflamed orifice.

Her scream was the last sound she made on planet earth.

15

Myth and Mystery

'The vaginal examination is essential for all obstetric and gynaecological diagnoses,' the professor's face was flushed and he was a little breathless as he turned to face the Grand Round.

One of the junior doctors approached the bed and placed a hand on the still wrist of Annelie Bormann. 'She's dead, sir.'

'Of course she's dead. Gentlemen, you see before you the final phase of puerperal fever.'

Semmelweis was outraged, he could only guess at the feelings of those around him. Some, he thought, felt this was just life and death in the maternity department, others, he hoped, were as profoundly upset as him.

'Would you like Mr Schweizer to present the differential diagnosis, sir?' Breit's voice was not confident.

'Of course not, the diagnosis is obvious.'

Poor Schweizer, dejected as his big moment was snatched away, gave a little formal bow and acknowledged, 'I understand.'

How ironic, thought Ignaz. He let slip a barely audible, 'Nobody understands.' Irma Valerie heard and gave him a murderous glare.

This one event brought home to Semmelweis the price these mothers paid for receiving free care in the hospital and allowing themselves to be used for the teaching of doctors. An exorbitant cost.

'Gentlemen, the cause of puerperal fever is in milk metastases. I have studied the subject extensively and there is no doubt in my mind that this is the nub of the matter.' The great man had quickly regained his composure. Moving the assembly around him away from the bed on which the dead Annelie was still lying, he went on, 'I have reluctantly set aside the miasmic and telluric theories that have held favour for so many years. Whatever may travel through the ether it is not puerperal fever.'

'Why is that, sir?' a courageous but incautious student enquired.

'Young man,' (pompous and patronising), 'have you seen objects flying through the air clearly labelled puerperal fever?'

'No, sir.'

'Gentlemen, breast milk in some women leaks into the blood stream and passes in small fragments to various parts of the body, where it lodges in small blood vessels cutting off the nourishing elements to the tissues.' Klein produced a smug grin. '*Quod erat demonstrandum.*'

'Sir, how do you reconcile your theory with the phlogistic or inflammation thesis of Karl Naegele in Heidelberg, who claims the process of puerperal fever originates in the fallopian tubes and ovaries?'

'Your name, sir?' Imperious, he did not recognize the visitor.

'Gottfried Eisemann of Würzburg.'

Semmelweis had heard of this physician who had written widely on medical and political matters. It was rumoured that he had supported the oppressed Hungarians in the Empire.

'Ha ha! The wizard of Würzburg in bed with the harlot of Heidelberg.' The insult stunned the whole room, doctors, nurses and mothers. 'It is obvious that puerperal fever is milk metastases.'

In this highly charged atmosphere Ignaz took a deep breath and began, 'Professor, sir, may I make two observations from my readings?'

'If you must.' Johann Klein was very irritable, no one knew of his forthcoming lunch date with the voluptuous wife of the Bulgarian ambassador.

'Although the work of Alexander Gordon of Aberdeen published in 1795 has largely been forgotten, he did report similarities between the illness of a doctor who accidentally cut his finger while dissecting a putrid body, and puerperal fever.'

'The men wear skirts in Scotland, they're all mad.' There seemed no end to Klein's invective, 'I hope there is no more of this nonsense, Doctor Semmelweis.'

'Sir, I would be grateful if your good self and the university department you so ably direct, would consider the paper of Oliver Wendell Holmes, published in Boston in April 1843.' Ignaz knew he was being outrageously obsequious and wondered if he could keep it up.

However, his strategy paid off immediately, 'Who is this Ven der Ohms?' Ignorance was on display.

'He is acting professor of anatomy at Harvard University in the United States of America.'

'Oh, that one, of course I know his writings well. No clinical experience, all theory, no fact.'

The young Hungarian doctor pressed on. 'Professor Holmes' treatise on contagiousness of puerperal fever suggests the disease is spread by contact, but does not explain how, when or where.'

'Not much of an explanation then,' the antagonism in the dialogue was returning.

Ignaz Fillipe Semmelweis, aspiring specialist physician in obstetrics, a Hungarian in Austria, trembled inwardly

63

but to all around was amazingly calm. 'Sir, this man made eight recommendations, firstly, that obstetricians should not perform post-mortem examinations on women who have died of puerperal fever.' He paused for a reaction. There was none but he could see the apprehensive expressions on his colleagues' faces. 'Secondly, if an obstetrician does do a post-mortem examination on such a woman who has died he should wash thoroughly, change all his clothes and wait twenty-four hours before performing a delivery.'

'Enough, enough,' Klein's face was puce, he was visibly trembling and spittle dripped from the corners of his mouth. He turned from the Grand Round assembly and stormed towards the door, Irma Valerie close on his heels. 'Complete rubbish,' could be faintly heard as he disappeared.

16

Birth of a Midwife

On the morning of New Year's Day, 1846 a small party stepped out and down the six steps of the Orlov house at number ten.

In this city music had reigned supreme since the extravagant days of Emperor Leopold I. At his marriage in 1666 to Infanta Margareta of Spain a 2,000-seat theatre had been built in the square of the Imperial Palace. The entertainment was *Il Pomo D'oro* (the golden apple), by Antonio Cesti. It was a lavish production with a cast of thousands, elephants and massive scenery machines.

For Charlotte this was a musical magical moment. She had worked hard and at an interview with the head midwife Suzanne Lafkrantz she had presented herself with great decorum and given an awesome impression of education and ability.

She had immediately liked the matronly chief nurse who took trouble to make her welcome and feel at ease. However, the presence of Irma Valerie holding her long black book, like a badge of office, was intimidating. There had not been a hint of recognition from the meddlesome controller, but Charlotte remembered her well with loathing.

She had been accepted readily by the midwifery school of the Vienna General Hospital and arrangements made for her to begin her training on the first day of 1846.

The morning was crisp and bright with a weak winter sun picking out the thick snow on the roofs, pavements and tops of the lamps of the open one-horse coach in which the small party was travelling.

Charlotte was holding baby Alexandra, opposite her sat Georgina with Edith beside her and Rudolf was proudly sitting beside his protégée.

The aspiring midwife once again wore the purple cloak left to her by her mother but this was now a very different garment. The thinned areas that had been repaired by some of the mothers in the first maternity clinic had been reworked extensively with new purple wool, giving a luxuriant thickness and weight for protection against the Vienna cold. There was now a brilliant white silk lining and around the hem a thick trim of white Arctic fox fur that nearly brushed the ground. The whole was crowned by a purple white-lined hood also trimmed with white fur. Finally the accessory of a white fur muff gave Charlotte a stunningly radiant appearance. Rudolf had provided the materials and Edith, Georgina and Charlotte had done the needlework, with Franz and Kate prancing around the workers giving encouragement and advice.

The carriage drew up outside the main entrance to the Vienna General Hospital. Charlotte kissed baby Alexandra, gave her one extra hug and handed her to Georgina's outstretched hands, kissed Edith's cheek and for the first time received a tender kiss on the cheek from Rudolf.

Placing his hand on her arm he said, 'Charlotte, you will do well, I know it, we all know it. Our thoughts and prayers will be with you.'

She stepped down and walked briskly towards the hospital. As she disappeared through the door surrounded by others she did not look back. Had she done so, she wondered if she would have carried on through the entrance.

Although she knew the way, as a result of her previous

very different arrival, she asked at the porter's lodge for directions to the second obstetric clinic.

'You don't even look pregnant, luv,' was the cheerful comment as she was pointed in the right direction.

She joined eleven other young women in the small lecture room adjoining the vast lying-in ward. Her fellow pupils were all wearing their best outfits.

Facing them on a dais with a lectern at each side were Suzanne Lafkrantz, the chief tutor midwife and Irma Valerie.

God, she's everywhere, thought Charlotte, and again the controller did not seem to know she had been a mother in the first obstetric clinic.

'Good morning, ladies,' beamed Suzanne, 'and welcome.' The homely buxom woman in her late forties continued, 'May I introduce Miss Irma Valerie, our controller, who will tell you about accommodation, uniforms and other social matters. You will address me as Tutor Suzanne,' she smiled. 'It should be Chief Tutor Midwife, but I think that's a bit pompous, don't you?'

There were polite little giggles in response. The tutor then moved on to the curriculum for pupil midwives. 'Your course will be for twelve weeks. During that time you will receive lectures in the mornings, practical instruction in the lying-in ward in the afternoon and in the evenings you will perform general nursing duties.

'From ten p.m. to twelve midnight you will study and memorise your lecture notes. You may then go to bed. Breakfast is at six-thirty, following this you may make your own beds, tidy your rooms and be in the lecture room at five minutes to eight o'clock.

'You will be instructed in the anatomy of pregnancy, the stages of labour and the midwife's role. You will receive lectures on the care of the newborn and the establishment of breast-feeding.

'These lectures will be given by me and members of my staff of tutors. You will also be lectured by the obstetric doctors and, of course, Professor Klein. In the second six weeks you will be expected to perform forty deliveries unsupervised.'

The pupils gave an, 'Ooh!'

Suzanne Lafkrantz turned to her left. 'I now hand over to the controller.'

Irma Valerie stepped forward with a brave effort of a smile: brave but not convincing. 'Good morning.' She could not manage 'ladies', or, 'welcome'.

'During your course you will all be resident in the nurses' home. You will each have a room, which you will keep immaculate at all times. There are no locks and meticulous inspections by me may take place at any time.'

The listening young women did not look pleased by the news but their faces fell even more as Irma Valerie continued. 'The only visitors you are allowed in your rooms are your colleagues sitting here today in this lecture theatre. No one from outside the hospital and definitely no men may enter your rooms.'

Irma Valerie's facial expression then changed to one of withering distaste. 'This brings me to the subject of medical students. Within this hospital, these overprivileged young men are the lowest form of life. They rank below the cockroaches in the kitchens. They are oversexed, frequently drunk, unwashed and their prime object for being here lies inside your knickers.'

There was no suggestion of humour in these remarks; Irma Valerie was in deadly earnest. 'You will be aware that medical students are confined to the first obstetric clinic and your midwifery training takes place in the second clinic. During your training you will not speak to, look at, think of and certainly not lust after any medical student. Any contact of any sort means instant dismissal.'

She spoke the last words with relish, separating each syllable to dis–miss–al.

'I now come to the awe-inspiring subject of our great director, Professor Johann Klein. He has, since his appointment in 1822, through hard work, brilliant research, outstanding diplomacy and supreme natural ability made this obstetric clinic the envy of the whole world. I will now conduct you to your rooms. Follow me.' Without any permission or acknowledgement of Tutor Suzanne, she strode from the room.

The new pupil midwives followed her out through the vast lying-in ward into the corridor. As they walked in pairs they passed Dr Ignaz Semmelweis talking to a colleague.

Semmelweis, whose memory was encyclopaedic, recognised Charlotte. He went up to her, walked beside her, 'It is wonderful to see my words fell on fertile ground.'

'You remember?'

'Of course.' He stopped walking, gave a little formal bow and Charlotte walked on.

17

A Word In Your Ear

Despite his undoubted power in the Vienna General Hospital and his influence at the Hofburg Palace, there was a man who struck fear in the heart of Johann Klein.

Karl Rokitanski, now aged forty-two, was twenty-six years younger than Klein who had been born in 1788. He was now professor in the Institute of Pathological Anatomy. A post he had held for the past two years.

His work involved the study of the appearance of diseased tissues and organs. Documentation was detailed, hand-written and laborious. He, personally, performed over 3,000 post-mortems each year.

He was a man of great integrity and at this stage of his career could not guess that he was destined to become rector of the University of Vienna and later chairman of the Austrian Academy of Sciences.

In recent months he had given permission and encouragement to the young obstetric extern from Budapest to work in the institute. He had been kind and friendly to Ignaz Semmelweis. He had more or less instantly heard of Klein's outrageous behaviour on the Grand Round the previous year and had received letters of protest from his counterparts in Heidelberg and Würtzburg. He felt sure other such letters had been received by his colleagues. As a result he now took a keen interest in the maternity department. He had also discussed the matter with Joseph Skoda, who was expected to be appointed professor of internal medicine later that year.

After the debacle of the now infamous Grand Round had been reported to him in detail he had taken the trouble to do some research on Ignaz Semmelweis. Everything he discovered about the young Hungarian doctor impressed him.

He had also read the relevant published works of Oliver Wendell Holmes. In particular he wanted to discover the remaining six of the eight recommendations for obstetricians that Ignaz had been prevented from making known.

He had discovered that post-mortems for erysipelas and peritonitis required the same preventative routines as those for puerperal fever. Points four, five, and six referred to doctors having affected women in their care and the suspension of their obstetric activity for up to a month.

The seventh concerned the duty of all staff to take hygienic precautions. However, what made the bespectacled, slightly balding Rokitanski's eyebrows shoot upwards was the final item.

Holmes had written that, 'Until the present time ignorance had been indulged, now it should be considered a crime.'

Rokitanski also knew that a vacancy had arisen in the midwifery unit for a lecturer appointment and that Semmelweis had applied again for the job. In light of recent events he felt sure Klein would oppose the Hungarian. It was now the second of February 1846 and the selection was due to be made on the twenty-seventh.

He took the unusual step of demanding, by letter, that the head of the maternity department should attend his office in the Pathology Institute the following day.

Klein was furious when he read the formally written

request. His initial response was to ignore the whole thing. On reflection he felt that this could cause him a lot of trouble and he wrote a note of reluctant acceptance which was delivered to the institute by Irma Valerie.

The portly professor entered Rokitanski's office without knocking on the door. He was deliberately twenty minutes late for the eleven o'clock meeting.

'Come in, come in, Johann,' the pathologist forced friendliness into his voice from behind his desk. 'Please take a seat.' A large, well-upholstered chair had been borrowed for the occasion. Klein sat down.

'What do you want?' The tone was truculent.

'A word in your ear,' he replied, smiling.

'I haven't got time for frivolities.' Klein was suspicious.

'I will come to the point directly. I believe you are appointing a new lecturer in your department on the twenty-seventh day of this month.' The pathologist was still smiling.

'That is true, but it has nothing to do with you or the Pathology Institute.'

Karl Rokitanski said nothing. He picked up the letters of complaint from Würzburg and Heidelberg and slid them across the desk towards Johann Klein. The smile had vanished. 'Read,' he instructed, the voice a little less friendly.

Klein took the papers and scanned over them briefly and then more carefully. His normally ruddy complexion turned to a deathly white. The language about him had been colourful indeed.

'Poppycock,' he blustered.

'It is not and you know it.' There was now an iciness in his voice. 'Details of that debacle of a Grand Round last year were reported to me in full.'

'They're lying.'

'I don't think so.'

72

'What do you want?' The good professor was now pleading and whining.

'On twenty-first June last year you did not appoint Dr Ignaz Semmelweis lecturer in your department. He was clearly the best candidate.'

'He was not,' Klein took a deep breath. 'He's a foreigner, he's always around spying and interfering. I don't like him. In the opinion of the interviewing committee Dr Franz Breit held a superior claim. It was unanimous.'

Karl Rokitanski was unmoved. 'You omit to mention that the meritorious Dr Breit is well connected with the royals.'

'He may be.'

'The new lecturer post: you will interview but you will not appoint Dr Semmelweis. Is that correct?'

'It is, so what? If you think I am going to select that little meddler Semmelweis, you can think again.' Klein was now bombastic.

'What I am thinking, is that the *Vienna Medical Weekly Journal* would be very pleased to publish those two letters.'

The professor's face turned white, 'Oh!' was all that came out.

'You are not a complete fool, Johann. You know how to prevent the contents of those graphic epistles from becoming public knowledge.'

The maternity department chief stood up and as rapidly as possible scurried out of Karl Rokitanski's office.

18

Fixed

Irma Valerie's ritual preparation for the appointments committee was the same as it had been in the previous June. However, the date on the wall read 27 February 1846.

Her dress was the same black ensemble but on her face there was a look of profound distaste. It seemed as though the stench of rotting flesh had just wafted across her finely pointed nose.

Klein had confided in her. 'I decided to go and see young Rokitanski about our new lecturer post.' His fabrication continued, 'We had a friendly discussion and decided Semmelweis was the best man for the job.'

She was flattered that he had divulged this information but horrified by his selecting the foreigner. Giving her ridiculous little curtsy, 'Very wise, Professor,' was her fawning response. It was difficult to hide her lack of enthusiasm.

Once again there were five short-listed doctors for the lecturer's appointment, which was so very essential for a career in obstetrics. None of them knew that this coming interview was a farce. The outcome had already been fixed.

These young men, together with Ignaz Semmelweis, had spent three days in the maternity department of the Vienna

General Hospital. They had attended ward rounds, introduced themselves to other doctors working in the first clinic and to senior midwives in the second unit. They all had high hopes, were dressed in their best suits and had recently had their hair and moustaches neatly trimmed.

There were three newly qualified Austrians with little or no postgraduate experience. They had all been astonished to find their names on the list. They had assumed that Austrian nationality and their high opinion of themselves were the deciding factors.

The fifth member of the group was Hungarian. Ignaz Hirschler, he was twenty-three years old, recently a doctor of medicine and interested in eye diseases. He was also a friend of Semmelweis. He had been utterly amazed at this turn of events and thought there must have been a mistake. He was wrong.

Klein had selected this quintet with care, excluding other better-qualified applicants.

The previous evening Ignaz Semmelweis had sat with Lajos Markusovszky in their small apartment. 'I am not hopeful; Klein hates me.'

'He may do, especially after that Grand Round fiasco, but you have good friends in the hospital,' Lajos replied. 'Your work is admired, you are well liked as a courteous, industrious and a very human being.'

'I thank you for your kind words, Lajos. I believe it is my duty to investigate the cause of puerperal fever,' he gloomily went on. 'Without my being appointed to this new post I can do nothing.'

'Have courage, my friend, all may not be as it seems.'

The following morning Ignaz had set off for the interview with a heavy heart.

The committee consisted of the same members as the previous June. It was Klein's choice; he did not like Skoda but knew he was close to Rokitanski. It would look very suspicious if he left him out.

The five applicants arrived in good time in the small waiting area outside the hospital boardroom. Irma Valerie swept in imperiously and made her usual pompous speech followed by, 'Dr Hirschler will be interviewed first, Dr Semmelweis next and then you three Austrian gentlemen, since you are all Von something.' The 'Von' denoted aristocratic but lowly.

Her comical curtsy brought smiles and she conducted Dr Hirschler into the adjoining room.

He returned after a respectable twenty minutes. He looked cheerful but not confident.

Without even speaking to him Irma Valerie pointed at Ignaz and then at the door leading to the committee. There was no curtsy. He followed her with a purposeful stride.

'Good morning, Dr Semmelweis,' Professor Klein boomed. 'Irma Valerie, please give our esteemed colleague a nice soft cushion for that awful hard chair.'

'Good morning, Professor,' Ignaz gave a slight formal bow, smiled and acknowledged the other members, 'Sirs.'

The cushion was slow to appear but eventually was placed on the seat. The inwardly apprehensive but outwardly calm young Hungarian sat down.

'Well now, doctor, how have you been getting on in my department?'

Semmelweis had prepared himself carefully for this occasion. He had ruled out any mention of O.W. Holmes. Instead he had decided to concentrate on his post-mortem and lecturing work.

'Sir, Professor,' he paused as Klein smiled at his colleagues. 'I have been performing post-mortem examinations on women who have died of puerperal fever. I have observed that many of them have a thick, foul-smelling fluid lying in the abdominal cavity.'

'Very interesting, doctor.' The committee chairman was desperate to avoid controversy and tried to change direction. 'Dr Von Welden, from the head of the university's office, perhaps you have a question?'

'What do you know about bee keeping?' The arrogant snob kept on jeeringly, 'it's a passion of mine.'

'Absolutely nothing.'

'Pity, no more enquiries.' The administrator was already bored.

To everyone's surprise the elderly Anton Schroeder was very much awake. 'Tell me about your post-mortem studies.' Klein forced a nod of approval for him to continue. 'What else have you observed, young man?'

'I have noticed swelling in the intestines and liver as well as the uterus.'

Ignaz had no reason to know that one of Anton's pupils had told him all about the well-liked Hungarian. He encouraged him, 'Go on.'

'I have carefully noted all my findings in detail and intend to study them for consistencies.'

'Quite right, young man. Never jump to conclusions. Statistical analysis is a great part of the future of medicine; it will leave old men like me out of date.'

'Sir, I know you have helped many aspiring doctors and are greatly appreciated.'

The white-haired man smiled, leant back in his chair, closed his eyes but did not snore.

19

Appointed

Von Hebra and Skoda had been impressed and exchanged a few whispered words.

'May I? Chairman?' Von Hebra, deeply involved in the classification of skin diseases, was given a slight hand movement of approval. 'Have you made any other discoveries, Dr Semmelweis?'

'It is not my observation but that of Professor Kolletschka. The infants who have died with their mothers from puerperal fever go to his forensic pathology department. He has noticed the same offensive fluid in some of their abdominal cavities.'

'Fascinating.'

Professor Skoda joined in the discussion, 'What else have you and Professor Kolletschka talked about?'

'As I am sure you remember, the smell from the post-mortem room, how it clings to clothes and especially to our hands. It is truly foul.'

'I do indeed, it was a very good reason to become a chest physician. Please continue,' the tone was cheerful and reassuring, the smile friendly and Ignaz felt a wave of confidence sweep over him.

'The professor puts oil on his hands and arms before work and washes in water that has had chlorine gas bubbled through it after post-mortem examinations.'

'And the result?'

'I have followed his procedure and although the odour is somewhat pungent the cadaveric stench is largely eliminated.'

'Do you think this has a place in the clinical situation?' Skoda liked the investigative mind of this young man.

'I have considered it, sir, but the tissues of the woman who is in labour or who has just given birth are bruised and sensitive – the chlorine might be damaging. Hand washing alone may be appropriate.'

Von Welden interrupted rudely, 'Chlorine gas is very expensive, is it not?'

Semmelweis did not get the opportunity to reply. Klein wanted to change the direction this interview was taking. He could not see himself doing all this hand washing. 'This position of aspirant lecturer does of course have a teaching role, doctor. Would you be kind enough to tell us about your experience in this function?'

'Sir, I am pleased to tell you that I have prepared and given lectures to both medical students and pupil midwives. They have included the anatomy of pregnancy, normal labour and delivery.'

'Excellent, young man,' Klein was benevolent. 'I don't think there are any more questions gentlemen?'

No one spoke but Semmelweis noticed that not only was Anton Schroeder not snoring, he was not breathing. He rose, walked around the table and held the wrist of the much-loved doctor. 'Sir, this man has just died.'

There were looks of profound surprise on all the faces around the table. 'A sad loss,' murmured Skoda. There were nods of assent.

'That will be all, doctor.' The shocked chairman indicated the door and the young Hungarian respectfully withdrew with a slight formal bow.

After the door closed Professor Klein spoke quietly,

'Irma Valerie, announce a short interval and arrange Dr Schroeder's removal.'

'Of course.' No curtsy, she hastened from the room.

There was little conversation in either room as Irma Valerie's arrangements were put in place. After the body had been removed as discreetly as possible by two burly mortuary attendants, on a wheelchair with a blue sheet over his head, there was a five-minute delay while all involved regained their composure.

The interviews of the remaining candidates took place in a subdued atmosphere and it was clear none of them were yet suitable for the job in question.

'Chairman,' said Josef Skoda when the door closed on the last one, 'I speak for both Dr Von Hebra and myself and say that Dr Semmelweis is the outstanding applicant here and has our vote.'

'Agreed, agreed.' In spite of the events of the morning the great man still had an appetite for his lunch date. 'Dr Von Welden, have you any views?'

'I don't like Hungarians but bow to the opinions of my colleagues.'

'A unanimous decision, excellent. Irma Valerie kindly invite Dr Semmelweis back to see us.'

She could not hide her disapproval as she did as she had been asked.

'Doctor Semmelweis, the committee has decided in its great wisdom to appoint you as aspirant lecturer in the maternity department of the Vienna General Hospital commencing today. Providing you perform well the regular post will be confirmed on the first of July 1846.'

Ignaz bowed, 'Thank you, gentlemen.' He turned and left. His smile was irresistible as he hurried off to find Lajos Markusovsky in the surgery department.

20

Charlotte's Progress

Lying on a table beside Tutor Suzanne was a beautiful wax model of the torso of a pregnant woman. It had been constructed with great skill and attention to detail by doctors in the Imperial Army. Many such life size works of human anatomy had been assembled to demonstrate the various systems of the body. Each item had taken eighteen months to produce using cadaveric dissections as a guide to display every aspect of nature's masterpiece. There were replicas of all systems, including new studies such as lymph vessels and glands, amounting to nearly one hundred specimens. The piece in front of the pupil midwives showed a vertical section of a baby in the uterus, with the head lying in a fully dilated cervix.

'Ladies, we have now reached the second stage of normal labour,' Suzanne's smile was that of a professional who truly enjoyed her job. Her inner tragedy was that she had never given birth herself.

She enthusiastically pointed to the widely open neck of the womb, the baby's head lying in the true bony pelvis of the mother and birth about to take place.

Charlotte was now at the end of her fourth week as a pupil midwife. She had worked hard each day and had fallen into an exhausted, deep but refreshing sleep at midnight.

She did, of course, miss Alexandra but her Sunday afternoon visits home gave her the contact she longed for daily. She was also reassured by the loving care her child was receiving.

She had been thrilled to learn about the growth and development that took place in the uterus, the onset of foetal movements and the stages of labour. As far as she could tell none of her eleven colleagues had given birth and certainly none had had her dreadful experience.

For all of them the afternoons were the most stressful. They were close to the mothers. Many of them had straightforward births with which they helped the duty midwives. Many recovered well but there was ever-present the terror of childbed fever.

These young women soon recognized the danger signals of fever with profuse sweating, abdominal pain and foul vaginal discharge. Hours were spent with cold sponges, soothing words and changing of bed linen. In spite of their efforts they were confronting death on a daily basis.

This had a huge impact on young minds. 'Surely there must be something that can be done about this terrible plague?' The tears rolled down the cheeks of Gisela Ehlers. A few minutes earlier she had tended the dying moments of yet another woman whose young life had ended in puerperal fever.

She sat with Charlotte in their little rest room at the side of the lying-in ward. They were both drinking a glass of warm water. A comforting arm around the shoulders of the sobbing girl had a calming effect.

Charlotte felt her own experience in the first obstetric clinic gave her insight into her colleague's feelings but not a sense of superiority.

'Gisela, we are here to train as midwives. During that time we are bound to witness horrors complicating childbirth. Childbed fever is at the front of our minds, our tutors' minds and at our early stage of knowledge and experience we must believe that doctors also share our concern.'

'Thank you, Charlie.'

'Nobody has called me that for a long time, but I like it.' She dimly recalled her arrival at the Vienna General Hospital just over eight months ago.

The days and weeks passed quickly and the twelve young minds quickly absorbed their teaching, and sadly accepted the deaths of the mothers and babies that occurred with such regularity.

The hospital grapevine was no different in the mid-nineteenth century from that which exists today. The news of the appointment of Ignaz Semmelweis as aspirant lecturer on 27 February had reached the school of pupil midwives later the same day. It was greeted with approval and enthusiasm, although there was an element of surprise. His first lecture to the young women was anticipated with excitement.

Tutor Suzanne preceded the recently selected lecturer into the small classroom. 'Doctor Semmelweis is already well known to you all. He is a great support to us midwives when we encounter complicated pregnancies and deliveries.'

She turned towards the slight, fair-haired figure beside her. 'Our guest speaker this morning is, at our own request, giving us a review of the scourge of childbed fever. We are all puzzled, distressed and horrified when we see young mothers die in pain, delirium and stripped of dignity. We have to stand by and provide comfort, but no remedy.'

She stepped down from the dais and all eyes turned towards the Hungarian. He knew it was a small audience, but felt they were the key to the future, working at the cutting edge of maternity care.

'Ladies, it is an honour to address you at this time of

agony throughout the great maternity hospitals of Europe and North America. The focus of attention for our branch of the caring profession has to be childbed fever.' As he finished his introductory remarks there was complete silence in the room. He had their undivided attention.

Instinct told him now was not the time for polemics, history lessons or theories dreamt up in ivory towers. He took a deep breath.

'Childbed fever is here in this maternity department and in all others. We do not know why it affects labouring women and their babies. We do not know how it is spread and we do not know how to prevent it happening.'

His most attentive and interested listener was Tutor Suzanne. The statements were, to her ears, a new and revolutionary kind of thinking.

'We are making progress, we need scientific investigation and change. There is already evidence that cleanliness has an important role to play.'

Semmelweis knew he was about to tread on dangerous ground. 'I intend to find out why only one per cent of Vienna mothers died of childbed fever fifty years ago.' His attentive audience was silent, unaware of the huge significance of his last words.

Tutor Suzanne Lafkrantz knew this was important, she did not know why.

Charlotte, who had experienced childbed fever but survived, listened intently. Her twelve-week course was passing quickly and in her mind she was totally committed to midwifery. She saw before her a slightly built fair-haired young man with twinkling blue-grey eyes, a foreigner from a country in the Austro-Hungarian Empire that was definitely treated as inferior. What she also saw was hope.

21

Ignaz' Progress

Monday 8 March 1846 was a crisp sunny morning at 8.15 a.m. when Semmelweis entered the first obstetric clinic. He had come from the autopsy room where he had adopted Kolletschka's practice of rubbing oil into his hands and forearms up to the elbows before making a post-mortem examination. Following the dissection of another victim of childbed fever he had washed with soap and water using a scrubbing brush for his nails, followed by *liquida chlorina*, which left his skin with a clean, fresh smell.

Kolletschka had not been mistaken; the solution was not sodium hypochlorite, as suggested by some doctors, but chlorine gas passed through water. However, the effect on the smell of decaying matter was as dramatic as he had said.

The pleasing hygienic aroma made Ignaz cheerful and there was a spring in his step. The day went well, healthy mothers and babies went home but at 4.15 p.m. a fracas broke out at the entrance and he hurried to find what only could be described as a brawl.

He halted in amazement. Fists were flying, feet kicking in all directions and 'You rotten bitches!' and 'Shut up, cow!' and 'Take your bloody hands off me!' were being screamed in soprano pitch.

'Ladies, please!' The normally gentle and calming voice was firm and incisive. 'What is going on?'

It had the required effect, the mêlée abruptly ceased and three bedraggled women slowly got to their feet.

There stood a breathless Ida and Gisela with a heavily pregnant woman between them. 'I am in labour and want to go into the second clinic. I have no wish to die in the first one.'

'We told her,' Gisela said, 'and then she started screaming, kicking and punching.'

'What did you tell her?' Ignaz watched the three women exchanging hostile glances.

'Why, that it's Monday and the second clinic's Sunday duty admissions stopped at four o'clock. She's got to go to the first one, rules is rules.'

The woman wailed. 'The head's coming. I should know – it's my third.'

A passing pupil midwife in her smart blue-striped uniform with a clean, white, neatly-pressed apron halted at the scene.

'Come, nurse,' Ignaz recognized Charlotte, 'take one arm and help me take her to the delivery room.'

'But I'm still only a pupil.'

'Never mind,' he replied more firmly.

She did as she was asked and together they hurried the moaning mother from the entrance.

'I know I'll die.'

'No you won't,' Charlotte soothed. 'What is your name?'

'Gunda, oh!' she grunted, as another contraction gripped her.

They reached the delivery area and Charlotte helped her up on to the table. She noticed the neat repair patches on the skirt. As yet another contraction and a louder, 'Oh, oh!' occurred as Charlotte gently coaxed her on to her left side, lifted the clothes free and pressed her knees up towards her chin, she was curled up in a ball.

A ball, but a dignified one, thought Semmelweis. 'Carry on, Charlotte. No protests about being only a pupil.'

There were no protests; she put a restraining right hand on the presenting head and a firm left hand on the distended belly. To Semmelweis' delight the delivery of a baby boy was conducted, beautifully, carefully and tenderly by the young woman.

After the cord was clamped, tied and cut Charlotte turned the mother on to her back, gave her the already wrapped baby to hold and awaited the afterbirth.

'Will I have to walk to the lying-in ward in three hours?'

'Is that one of your fears of the first clinic?'

'Yes.'

'I will carry you.'

The contractions returned. Charlotte separated the mother's bent knees and gently eased the placenta and some blood into a kidney-shaped porcelain dish. She cleaned her vulva with warm water and placed a small white towel over the so very recently stretched tissues. The skirt of patches was restored to its place.

The peace and happiness of the room was shattered by a furious hammering on the door, which was not locked. 'Where is my delivery?'

An unshaven, dishevelled young man burst in. 'I am the student assigned the next one.'

Seeing Charlotte and the baby lying in his mother's arms his face turned purple with rage. 'You've stolen my case,' he screamed at the young midwife.

Semmelweis was outraged; he took hold of the student's shoulders, turned him and propelled him back through the door: no mean feat, as the student was a good six inches taller than him. 'Go home, wash, sober up and come to see me in six hours.'

The only person not shaking after this unpleasant episode

was the baby, still lying peacefully. His experience of planet earth was less than one hour.

Ignaz placed an arm around the still quivering Charlotte's shoulders. 'Tutor Suzanne can be proud of you. A perfect delivery.'

A warm glow spread through her. She felt she was now a midwife, although her course still had another twenty-one days to run.

Three hours later Semmelweis carried Gunda and her son to the lying-in ward. Three hours after that, the medical student did not come to see the young Hungarian obstetrician.

22

Tables

Lajos Markusovsky entered the apartment he shared with Semmelweis and was assailed by the characteristic musty odour of old books and papers.

He looked around him and saw piles of dusty, dirty old files. They were stacked on tables, chairs, bookshelves and most of the floor space. In the middle of all this, sleeves rolled up, bow tie undone sat his friend with a broad smile lighting up his face.

'Lajos, welcome to the obstetric department of the Vienna General Hospital, opened in 1789.'

'Fascinating! Where can I sit?'

'Ah, just put 1802 on top of 1801 and your favourite chair is instantly available.'

'How did you get all this stuff here?'

'From a very unlikely source of assistance.'

'I can't see your good professor getting his hands dirty or straining his back for your benefit.'

'Quite right. You remember the medical student I told you about?'

'The dirty drunken one who was late for the delivery?'

'Exactly. He eventually came to see me. In fact he is a very nice young man called Flor Balassa, nephew of Janos who became professor of surgery in Pest three years ago.'

'Friends in high places?'

'Not really. He apologised profusely for what he said was unforgivable conduct. He has also apologised to both Charlotte, the pupil midwife, and Gunda, the mother involved in the incident.'

'Did he volunteer to bring all these records here?'

'Not quite, he did feel offering me some form of assistance might restore his position. I noted he had broad shoulders and strong arms, I thought they should be put to good use.'

'Are we going to live in this mouldy archive for a long time?'

'Oh no. Flor has already returned 1789 to 1797 to the hospital basement.'

'My lungs are very pleased about that. What exactly is all this going to produce?'

'Tables.'

Lajos raised his eyebrows. 'I'll avoid the obvious pun about your carpentry skill and let you explain.'

'It's really quite simple.' Ignaz' enthusiasm pushed Lajos' discomfort into the background.

'I'm recording all the deaths from childbed fever since the hospital opened. The year, the month and total numbers of deliveries.'

'That's a huge job.'

'I thought it would be, but I'm grateful to Professor Lucas Boer. He was in charge of the obstetric department for thirty-three years and a great reformer.'

'Remind me.' Lajos knew the name but not the details.

'He believed in natural childbirth. No purges, no blood letting and very little interference. The result, very little paperwork. I have not yet reached 1822 when he retired but I think his deaths from childbed fever were fewer than we have now.'

'That's amazing,' Markusovsky was impressed. 'Can you explain it?'

'No,' Ignaz was grateful for his friend's excitement. 'I believe these tables will show us where to look for the cause of childbed fever.'

'Ignaz,' said Lajos, 'I admire your devotion to the poor ladies who die of childbed fever, but surely other obstetricians not only here in Vienna but in the rest of Europe and the world have sought to solve the problem.'

'Oh, they have! Karl Carus here in Vienna proclaimed it a revolution in the female body in 1829, Dietrich Busch of Leipzig thought in 1843 it was due to pressure of the pregnant uterus on adjacent organs, and in the last few months Wilhelm Scanzoni of Würzburg has declared that in pregnancy there is a rise in the fibrin in the blood, called hyperinosis, causing exudates on the peritoneum.'

'That was quite a speech. What makes you think they could be wrong?'

'They are theories, dreamed up in their palatial offices.'

Markusovsky's luxuriant eyebrows shot up. 'They're all top men, leaders in their field, professors and departmental heads.'

'I know, and so is our Professor Johann Klein,' Ignaz' tone was passionate and not vindictive. 'He subscribes to the most accepted and fashionable theory of all.'

'Which is?'

'Atmospheric, mysterious noxious vapours, a something from outside the body.'

'Ah ha, the famous miasma.'

'Exactly,' Semmelweis frowned. 'These men don't say if it's telluric, from planet earth or cosmic from the universe.'

'Apart from being theories have you anything else against these doctrines?'

'Don't you see, Lajos? They are accepted: that's it, end of story, mothers die in agony. Never mind the deprived husbands, children, sisters, brothers – it's all atmospheric.'

'I know you to be a man of great humanity but it won't

help your research if you become personally involved; in fact it will work against it.'

'You're right. I thank you for listening and your interest.'

'Have you ever thought why a professor is a professor?'

'Not really.' Ignaz recognized the wisdom of the change of direction of dialogue; passion was overriding reason.

'Well, take your Johann Klein, for example. He's not the super obstetrician his title would suggest, although his knowledge of pregnancy and its complications is extensive.'

'True enough, but where is all this taking us, Lajos?'

'He's been head of the obstetric unit for more than twenty-three years. What has sustained him?'

'It's not research or publication.'

'Agreed. The answer is students and administration. If the students like him, speak well of him and pass their examinations, he gets the government money and influence.'

Ignaz was curious. 'I suppose that means that he appoints lecturers who will toe the line.'

'Precisely.'

'Then why appoint me?'

'Because somebody, somewhere likes you.'

23

Graduation

The twelve pupil midwives of Charlotte's class were now dressed in the long, high-necked bright violet uniforms of staff midwives. For this formal occasion they had discarded their starched white aprons and were proud to no longer be wearing the blue and white stripes of a trainee. They walked in pairs down the centre aisle between the rows of proud families and friends and took their places at the front.

The conference room of the Vienna General Hospital was packed with people on this first day of April 1846. Before them was a table on the dais on which were twelve neatly rolled diplomas each tied with a pink ribbon. Beside the table was an easel supporting a gilt-framed portrayal of the 'Midwife's Oath' in a beautiful handwritten script, which read:

I, as a midwife solemnly swear in the presence of those gathered here:

I will comply with the laws of Austro-Hungary and my adequate behaviour will always be in harmony with my chosen profession.

To the best of my ability as a midwife I will improve my knowledge and develop my training to a high standard.

I will put all my efforts into helping physicians and others caring for patients.
I will keep secret and confidential all information obtained while performing my duties.
I will neither take nor give to others any harmful materials.
My actions, by personal example, are devoted to the health and welfare of the patients put in my care.

Sitting in the third row were Charlotte's new family, Rudolf Orlov, in a smart new grey suit especially made for the occasion with a white shirt and sky-blue bow tie. The smile on his lean face registered both pride and happiness but his eyes were moist at the memory of his Alexandra. It was on the day she died that, he remembered, he had last been inside the Vienna General Hospital. He briefly forgot the day he collected Charlotte.

Beside him was Edith with ten-month-old Alexandra asleep on her ample lap. Rudolf had had some misgivings about bringing the child but Edith had firmly reassured him, 'These are the people who bring children into the world.' There was no defence against such logic. Edith was also dressed for the occasion in turquoise jacket, long matching woollen skirt and a fine black broad-brimmed hat with white tulle trimming.

On her right were Georgina, Franz and Kate in their Sunday Best and eyes bright with excitement. At the back of the room sat Semmelweis, Markusovsky and a few other doctors. There was no sign of Klein. Irma Valerie stood unsmiling at the entrance.

A buzz of expectation electrified the room. There were rumours, this was more than the usual graduation ceremony. Intermittently, Franz's reciting of the Midwife's Oath could be heard above the hushed whispers. Kate pinched his thigh. 'Ouch!' became part of the pledge.

Suzanne Lafkrantz appeared from the side of the low stage in a midwife's dress with a grey cape over her shoulders.

She was followed by an amazing sight, greeted by 'Oohs!' and 'Aahs!' and 'It is her!' followed by enthusiastic applause.

Jenny Lind, the 'Swedish Nightingale', was a face that currently covered Vienna. It was on posters, in bookshops and art shop windows, on chocolate and cigar boxes, scented soaps and toilet waters. A perfume was labelled *extrait double de bouquet de Jenny Lind.*

Her appearance was stunning; her long scarlet skirt complemented a black lace high-neck long-sleeved blouse. Luxuriant blonde hair was piled high on her head and topped by a magnificent broad-brimmed scarlet hat with at least a dozen black ostrich feathers. The outfit was completed by a black furled parasol with an ivory handle. Her presence in Vienna was due to her starring role as Marie in Donizetti's *The Daughter of the Regiment.*

Her fame had preceded her, she had been fêted in London where Victoria and Albert had attended one of her performances; the Queen herself threw the first bouquet.

Semmelweis applauded as much as anyone else and greatly admired this vision of grace and beauty, whom he knew to be just two years younger than himself.

Suzanne held up her right hand and the room quietened immediately. 'I see Miss Lind is no stranger to any of you. She is, of course, our guest of honour and has kindly agreed to present our midwives' diplomas.'

Like others, Ignaz wondered how the diva had been persuaded to come to the hospital. There were hidden depths to Tutor Suzanne.

'Today we honour and congratulate twelve dedicated young ladies.' Suzanne's tone was both sincere and proud. 'To train as a midwife is not easy. It places physical and psychological stress on a young woman.'

She had her audience's attention. Jenny Lind, statuesque, watched and listened.

'The hours are long, the discipline rigorous and the commitment permanent. There is the joy of assisting a new life into this world and the supreme happiness seen on the face of a mother.'

She turned momentarily towards Jenny. 'We are one of the greatest teaching hospitals in the world; we train medical students to be doctors and some of the brightest young men to be obstetricians. Alongside them we train midwives who single-handedly deliver the babies and assist in the training of medical students. However, their skills also include the knowledge and judgement of what is not straightforward and the necessity for the obstetrician.

'Many of our mothers are poor, some unmarried and unsupported but most leave the hospital with their babies to face the future.

'However,' Suzanne's voice faltered, 'one of our great sadnesses remains childbed fever. Unexplained, difficult to treat and frequently fatal to mother and child, our midwives can only provide comfort and care.

'While I see it, my heart breaks but I am sure someone, somewhere will come to the aid of these unfortunate women. Meanwhile these young ladies will provide whatever they are able with love and compassion.' These words struck a deep chord in the conscience of Ignaz Semmelweis.

'Eight of our new midwives will be assigned to the first obstetric clinic and four to the second, but before that there will be one week of holiday,' Suzanne smiled. 'And now I ask Miss Lind to present the diplomas after I have read the Midwife's Oath.'

She read from the framed writing and then each of the graduate's names. One by one Jenny Lind presented the ribboned scroll to the elated women and acknowledged their curtsies.

'I cannot make a speech to such angels but I can sing for them.'

The whole room knew or hoped they knew what was coming. Unaccompanied, this glorious voice with great trills took on the role of Marie with the song of the regiment.

> All men confess it
> Go where we will
> Our gallant regiment
> Is welcome still.

24

The Midwife's Tale

They loved her, the audience was spellbound and when Jenny Lind finished she placed her arms around the shoulders of the two new midwives on each side of her.

With hands joined the whole group made a deep bow cum curtsy to wild rapturous applause. It was a joyous moment.

At last Rudolf gathered his party together and Charlotte made her adieus to her colleagues, Suzanne and Jenny Lind.

They passed through the crowd, received a beaming smile from Dr Semmelweis accompanied by a slight formal bow.

Outside the hospital was a two-horse open carriage. They climbed aboard, Alexandra smothered in kisses safe in Charlotte's arms.

There were gusts of wind but the cotton-wool white clouds did not threaten rain and as one of the many clocks in Vienna struck twelve o'clock warm sunshine bathed the happy passengers. Spring was in the air; the flowersellers did brisk business with daffodils, tulips and irises.

From the Vienna General Hospital their coachman drove up to Währinger Strasse and right into the tree-lined street.

They carried on past Maria Theresien Strasse where number ten and home prematurely awaited them. The two horses trotted on passing shops and cafés all of which had posters of Jenny Lind in their windows. Shortly before reaching the Hofburg Palace the carriage pulled to a halt outside Luigi's famous Italian restaurant. 'Celebration lunch,' announced Rudolf. There was delight and surprise on everyone's face. Once inside a handsome young man in green waistcoat, white shirt and black trousers conducted them to a table near the window. As he handed out the menus he gave Georgina a massive moustachioed smile with a mouthful of glorious white teeth. She blushed, Kate giggled and Franz pinched her thigh.

'Knowing my family they will read your *carte du jour* from cover to cover, meanwhile we will have some fruit juices and wine which I will ask you to select.'

'For the baby?' the waiter enquired.

'Edith has come prepared.' A package was produced and Alexandra gurgled a smile and began lunch.

'I can still hear that wonderful voice,' Edith enthused. 'What an amazing tribute to you and your colleagues, Charlotte.'

'Even now I can't believe it. Those trills, all of you there, I shall never forget this miraculous day! Rudolf, words are not enough to thank you.' She leaned across to where he sat beside her and gently kissed his cheek.

Those at the table clapped their hands, heads in the restaurant turned and in the quiet that followed Orlov's refined voice could be clearly heard. 'Charlotte, you are a credit to your midwife's uniform. We all congratulate you and wish you well for a successful professional future that brings happiness and fulfilment.'

Rudolf knew the moment was right, 'I cannot bring back my dearest wife, Alexandra whose sweetness you,

Charlotte, experienced for only a few hours, but you are a living, visible memorial to her.' The whole restaurant burst into applause.

Lunch arrived, steaming hot venison, gorgonzola sauce and all the trimmings that everyone had selected. A perfect choice and at the end the plates were completely clean. Content, united and exhilarated the party again boarded an open two-horse carriage. En route for home Kate whispered in Charlotte's ear, 'What is childbed fever? Is that why my mother died?'

Charlotte respected Kate's confidence and the innocence of a child. Very quietly she answered, 'Your mother died because her baby was in a position that prevented him being born. Usually it is treatable but everything happened too quickly. It is very uncommon; it was a tragedy.' Kate nodded her understanding.

Kate and probably her brother and older sister had hung on Tutor Suzanne's every word with their mother in mind. The questions deserved an honest answer. 'Childbed fever is sadly much more frequent. It is a very bad plague that seems only to affect women when they have a baby. Nobody really knows why it happens.'

The coach drew up in front of number ten and they all went in. Georgina, Franz and Kate thanked their father, hugged Charlotte and disappeared upstairs. Rudolf, Edith and the new midwife carrying her daughter sat down in the front room.

'Charlotte, in such a short time you have become a young professional woman in a world of amazing contrasts. New lives begun but many young mothers dying.'

'It is truly terrible. We watch young women die, we don't know the reason. The midwives do talk about these things although we accept our role as being lowly.'

Taking a deep breath, 'A lovely girl came into the second obstetric clinic two weeks ago. She had had labour pains two days earlier but they stopped and the doctors said that although she was past her delivery date the head was not engaged in the pelvis and she was sent home. Three days afterwards her waters broke and her contraction pains started again and were coming quite regularly when she came back.'

Charlotte could see Edith and Rudolf understood her story. 'She was examined and re-examined but the cervix was very slow to dilate, it was her first child. She remained labouring for another sixty hours, she started vomiting, could not keep food or water down and finally the cervix was judged to be fully dilated. A doctor applied the forceps and a very poorly baby came out with awful tearing of the vagina. She suffered so very much.'

She stopped, not knowing if her story was too upsetting. 'Go on,' said Rudolf.

'The afterbirth came easily and quickly and she kept down some water, but in two hours she had the fever, the shaking, the awful foul-smelling discharge and was in great pain, especially when we moved her. She died six hours after the birth and the poor child half an hour later.'

Edith spoke with sadness in her voice, 'There must be a reason why you are telling us this.'

'Of course, I have seen so little but the other midwives much more. It was such a long time and her poor flesh so badly cut and bruised. Some said she was bound to get the fever.'

Rudolf asked, 'Was anything else said?'

'There are so many rumours and it seems to make for bad feelings among the doctors.'

'Was anything said to Tutor Suzanne?'

'Angelica, a midwife who has been there many years, told her and said it had happened after other long labours she had seen. Suzanne said, "thank you, another sadness".'

Rudolf leaned back in his chair, 'Your compassion is right but you must remain strong.'

Difficult, very difficult, thought Charlotte.

25

Analytical Brain

Charlotte commenced her duties in the first obstetric clinic of the Vienna General Hospital on the ninth of April 1846.

She was immediately struck by the fervent activity of Dr Semmelweis. She saw he was not only performing his duties, teaching and resolving obstetric problems, but he was simply always there.

On more than one occasion she heard a doctor say, 'Semmelweis has changed from the carefree, cheerful student we once knew; he is now the most active and painstaking doctor in the hospital. He seems to be spurred on by the experience of childbed fever.'

One morning Charlotte identified a transverse lie in a newly admitted labouring mother; Ignaz Semmelweis was the doctor who came to their aid. She was only too well aware that this was the condition that killed Rudolf's Alexandra.

It was a rare predicament and students had gathered round. Labour was suppressed with laudanum and muscles were relaxed. Firmly, gently and slowly the baby was rotated within the uterus until the head was in the correct position.

'In the Vienna General Hospital we have over six thousand maternity admissions each year. Only between ten and fifteen have mal-presentations like this which are saveable when treated without delay.'

Semmelweis had the attention of students, midwives and doctors, 'Yet', he continued, 'many hundreds die of childbed fever.' He warmed to his theme. 'Medicine's highest duty is to save threatened life and we do succeed frequently, but when the fever strikes we seem to be powerless.'

No one spoke. 'We work in conditions of overcrowding, many of our patients are poor and undernourished, some through fear have sought the attentions of the abortionist and others give birth in the streets.'

'There is much to be done.'

Just how much was only fully seen by Lajos Markusovsky. In this period of 1846 Semmelweis assembled eighty tables of statistics from the hospital records of 1789 to 1846.

'Lajos, there are three dates that leap out of these figures: 1822, 1833 and 1839.'

'Not so very long ago.' The apartment had now been cleared of all the hospital records, which had been returned to the archives by the strong and still willing Flór.

The young surgeon stretched his long legs. 'It's good to have the apartment back. Tell me more.'

Semmelweis picked up the eighty sheets of figures, flipped through them and sat opposite his friend. 'For the first thirty-three years of our hospital, deaths from childbed fever remained more or less constant at one per cent. Then in 1822 the mortality rate steadily started to rise.'

'That is astonishing. By how much?'

'From about sixty to four hundred each year.'

'That is truly dreadful. What happened in 1833?'

'Nothing. That is to say no change in the appalling deaths from the fever, but the department was divided into first and second clinics by Professor Klein.'

'And 1839?' his colleague was really curious.

'In that year the second obstetric clinic was devoted only to teaching midwives. The medical students were confined to the first clinic and, here is the point, deaths in the second clinic have significantly fallen. In the last year there were four hundred and fifty-nine deaths in the first and only one hundred and five in the midwives' training clinic.'

'Amazing. My first reaction, Ignaz, is that you must publish this information, but I am sure you should delay and not expose yourself to damaging criticism.'

'Especially the wounded feelings of Johann Klein.'

In the following weeks Charlotte and others witnessed unannounced changes instituted by Dr Ignaz Semmelweis. Dominating his thinking was the startling difference in death rates between the first and second obstetric clinics, almost exclusively due to childbed fever.

On a teaching round a student presented a woman in labour. 'I liked your description of the findings in this lady on physical examination of the abdomen and pregnant uterus. However,' his tone was courteous, 'I would have liked it better if this woman had a name, an age, a past obstetric history, a record of previous illnesses and medications.' He was not finished. 'Have we a member of the human race with a family, home and occupation?'

'I quite understand, sir.' The student graciously accepted the gentle admonition.

'In what position will you deliver the baby?'

'Dorsal position, sir.'

'I would like you to try the lateral position, it is more dignified on her left with you attending her from the right side of the delivery couch.' He did not add that this was the position frequently used in the second clinic. 'You can, of course, always revert to the dorsal position if there is a problem.'

Turning to another student, 'What happens to the mother when her birth has been completed?'

A young man volunteered, 'After a three-hour rest she walks to the ward.'

Ignaz did not allow enthusiasm to dominate fairness. 'That is usual, but from now I ask all of you, students, midwives, assistants and doctors to help in carrying these, sometimes exhausted, women.'

At this time Professor Klein was rarely seen. His Grand Rounds were short, uncontroversial and dull but just long enough to show that he was still alive. Nevertheless the menacing presence of Irma Valerie was always there. She silently noted that Klein was being kept away from high-risk mothers. She looked on in amazement at the prospect of wealthy women, begging, wringing their hands, and even resorting to bribery in their attempts to be admitted to the second clinic rather than the first.

Semmelweis was constantly looking for differences that could be changed between the two clinics.

The priest, his entourage and the bell of doom were redirected in their mournful journey. Now, instead of passing through five rooms they only went via one to reach a deceased woman.

He also turned his attention to comparisons of diet, ventilation and laundry.

His curiosity extended to the home births conducted by midwives alone with apparently few complications.

Meanwhile there was little in the first obstetric clinic of the Vienna General Hospital that was not reported to Johann Klein by Irma Valerie.

106

26

Definitions

Semmelweis knew that his friend and ally Ferdinand Von Hebra was engaged researching the scratching disease that came to be known as scabies. It was widespread, and intense irritating sores caused immense misery among the poor and deprived populations of Europe.

He needed a mentor to put his thoughts in order.

They met in a coffee shop in Schubertgasse near the birthplace of the musician who had died in 1828.

'Ferdinand, I have looked at so many possible factors relating to childbed fever. I believe I know how it happens, but my thoughts are in turmoil.'

Von Hebra did not hesitate. 'I understand the difficulty very well. I am embarking on a classification of skin diseases and I find so much information but so much disorder.'

'My problem exactly.'

'We live in times of great change, there are stirrings of independence in the countries of the Austro-Hungarian Empire. In medicine, from my point of view, we are at the end of the era of unfounded speculative theories dreamed up in the comfort of ivory towers.

'Looking at the mortality rates in the first and second obstetric clinics has forced me to reach one single conclusion. Childbed fever is caused by decomposing organic material being transferred from the post-mortem room to the bruised and lacerated genitalia of previously healthy women after or during birth.'

'That is an astonishing statement.'

Semmelweis paused, drank his coffee and then continued, 'There was no eureka moment, it dawned on me slowly, and there is worse to come.'

Von Hebra's expression was grave. The words he was hearing were both amazing and dangerous, a risk to Semmelweis.

'I believe that contaminated particles are carried on the hands of doctors and medical students to a point of entry into the bloodstream of these unfortunate mothers.' Semmelweis was more confident now.

'And then?'

'And then the whole body becomes affected by exudates and abscesses.'

Dermatologist Von Hebra saw the point clearly. 'Childbed fever and death,' he said.

'Exactly, but at post-mortem the main focus of the process is in the region of the still enlarged and engorged uterus. There are frequently associated collections of pus in distant organs such as the brain, liver and lungs. The contaminated material can only have reached these structures via the bloodstream.'

'Have you discussed any of this with another person?'

'I showed my friend Markusovsky the records and the three key dates: 1822, 1833 and 1839. He said publication was tempting but would leave me open to great criticism.'

'You are young, you have certainly discovered something but the old guard is there. They will seize on any weakness to protect their positions, power and wealth.'

'What should I do?' He trusted Von Hebra.

'Test your theory against all that is known about this dreadful disease, particularly the ideas from the ivory tower department. If you will excuse me I have to leave. I wish you well, I am here if you need me.' He left giving Ignaz a smile of encouragement.

Many of the coffee shops in Vienna in those days were used to the needs of students and academics of the university. When he asked for pen and paper it was willingly and readily supplied.

After it arrived the young Hungarian stared at it while he sipped another coffee. It was not long before he separated five sheets of paper and wrote in large capital letters one word on each page. Very clear, very large and underlined were:

EXTERNAL
INTERNAL
EPIDEMIC
ENDEMIC
CONTAGION

As he looked at these important words he realised that there would be some crossover of the various factors under each heading, some blurring of the edges of these definitions.

He dealt with external influences first and started with his proposition. He wrote:

Decomposing matter from cadavers adheres to the hands, arms and clothes of doctors and students. It has a characteristic foul smell. These particles are introduced into the broken, damaged and bruised organs of the unfortunate women and from there to the blood circulation.

He felt that he had to write down what he had told Von Hebra and it helped to clarify his mind. He knew, that for him, learning was not only reading a book, casting it aside and thinking he had learned something. As a student and now as a doctor eternal repetition in his mind and on paper cemented and matured his knowledge and ideas.

The dramatic test of his proposition was the stunning difference in childbed fever between the first and second clinics. With this in mind he reviewed the other external factors.

Rough and multiple examinations, especially in prolonged labours, occurred in both clinics.

Street births were admitted for free treatment because it was felt the intention to come to the hospital was present and they were teaching subjects. The incidence of childbed fever was low and sometimes mild in these women but they are equally divided between both clinics.

Some women had travelled great distances, even from beyond the glacis, or slope, outside the city walls. Such women were in poor health but went to both halves of the maternity department.

Semmelweis was well aware that one of his newly qualified midwives had had a street birth and contracted a mild form of childbed fever from which she recovered. He did not know how or why.

He then turned to his page marked internal. In this group he listed all the circumstances that were present within the patient that might have an effect on childbed fever, but were not introduced from the exterior.

These included crushed tissue, particularly by the use of obstetric forceps, which had been introduced in 1723. Other devitalised tissue included retained parts of the placenta and, at its extreme, there was the intra-uterine death of a child. In these circumstances there were no differences between the two clinics.

However, his researches had shown that when there was prolonged labour and the cervix was fully dilated for more than twenty-four hours the first clinic had a worse record.

Where the babies were affected the changes at post-mortem were the same as in the mother except the genital area was not more severely affected.

Apart from the prolonged labour factor, which fitted in with Semmelweis' hypothesis, all the other aspects affected the whole maternity department in equal measure.

Epidemic was a term frequently and pointlessly applied to the problem. Of course childbed fever was widespread. Smallpox was epidemic but always gave smallpox to another previously healthy person in the same atmospheric environment. Childbed fever was a disease that had many different features with many organs affected. There was no difference in the atmospheres of the two units.

There were epidemic features such as a low incidence of the disease in holiday periods. The authorities had recognised this and concluded the disease was due to rough foreign students, such as Hungarians, who they banned for some time. This did not alter the disproportionate incidence; likewise the weather was the atmosphere and common to them all.

And so he came to the page marked endemic, in other words regular local conditions that might have an adverse influence. Overcrowding, poor ventilation and old buildings were the same for both; in fact the first obstetric clinic had been built more recently.

The poor circumstances of the patients were equally divided and in fact the fever problem was much more prevalent in the Vienna General Hospital than the city at large.

There was a common ante-room, the lateral position was now in use in the first clinic and the walk three hours after delivery was now changed. In fact it had been a much longer walk in the second clinic.

Hygienic measures were the same for both and at this point Semmelweis noted that only chlorine washings could eliminate the smell of putrefaction. The laundry of the whole department was mixed in with that of the general hospital.

Diet, affront to modesty and fear all operated throughout in similar ways and even the priest's bell had been eliminated. There was some staff disrespect and Ignaz Semmelweis felt it personally after he had made changes.

Finally, this painstaking doctor addressed the subject of contagion. He had to be very clear why childbed fever was not a contagious disease in which there was direct contact between an affected patient and a healthy mother. This simply did not take place even though women in rows of beds could be affected. There was no touching or bodily contact.

He was finished; he read what he had written. There was only one possible conclusion from all of this.

Putrefying, decaying, decomposing animal organic matter was transferred by the hands and clothes of doctors and students to the damaged genital areas of mothers. From there it entered the blood.

He shuddered. How many cases were there in which Ignaz himself had been the instrument of death?

27

Victimisation

Irma Valerie had assumed the roles of spy and conspirator with no difficulty at all. It was made exceedingly easy by her dislike of Semmelweis, a foreigner, a Hungarian and an apparently tireless worker.

In late September 1846 he was struck by the plight of the foreign students who had been banned by the authorities from working in the first obstetric clinic.

He introduced a small pilot scheme of chloride of lime hand washing for all those doctors and students performing post-mortems and then attending women in labour.

He had turned from *liquida chlorina* to chlorinated lime, also known chemically as calcium hypochlorite, because of expense. Both have a clean, refreshing smell and release oxygen, as demonstrated by Bethollet in 1785.

For ease of terminology he called this 'chlorine hand washing'. Medical students have notoriously found chemistry and physics a difficult part of their academic training.

As September passed, Semmelweis produced for the authorities figures showing a modest fall in the mortality rates in the first clinic.

He was not comfortable with such a small imprecise trial but officialdom relented and the foreign medical students were allowed back into the first obstetric clinic for their two-month courses.

Irma Valerie was outraged and stormed into Professor Klein's office. 'This, Professor, is the last straw.' She threw down the document from the university administrators which re-admitted students from outside Austria.

Klein did not take kindly to this explosive interruption but he knew she was his eyes and ears. 'Irma Valerie, a little decorum, please.' He cast his eyes over the directive.

'He's meddlesome, bypasses your authority and is a Hungarian.' She was slowly regaining her composure. 'He has to go.'

'You're right, I will dismiss him. His interfering has gone far enough. You will present him with this note terminating his appointment today, twentieth of October 1846.'

He wrote an insultingly brief letter to Dr Semmelweis discharging him from his duties. It was not even sealed. He handed it to his devious collaborator.

She took it gleefully, 'You give no reason?'

'Why should I?' Johann Klein was beginning to realise the threat to him posed by the Hungarian lecturer in his department. 'He goes his own way, he has not sought my permission for any changes and I will not humiliate myself by giving a reason for his dismissal.'

The sallow-faced calculating controller was finding it difficult to hide her delight at this turn of events. 'Who will do his work?'

'Dr Breit can take over and there are those young Austrian doctors we interviewed who will be very pleased to be called upon in this,' he paused, there was no suitable word, and he settled for, 'emergency.'

Irma Valerie gave one of her absurd little curtsies and scuttled off on her poisonous assignment.

Ignaz Semmelweis was tired by the combined effect of both his duties and his researches. He did, however, have a fragile optimism when Irma Valerie handed him Klein's curt note. He was shattered and dispiritedly made his way home. Fortunately Markusovsky was already in the apartment.

When he appeared looking so dejected his friend thought it was due to the news of Ignaz' father having died a week earlier. 'The loss of your father sits heavily on your shoulders tonight, old friend.'

'No it's not that, although it saddens me greatly. I have been dismissed from my job.'

Lajos Markusovsky was horrified. 'What misdemeanour or grounds were cited?'

'None,' Semmelweis replied wearily. 'That harpy Irma Valerie merely handed me an open scrappy note from Klein. She was derisive and triumphant.'

'She has always disliked you for being a Hungarian and regards your activities as a threat to the old guard.' Lajos' indignation was fierce but he felt he must give positive support. 'Be patient, my good friend. You are widely admired by doctors, students and nursing staff. Your dedication, particularly to suffering women, is unsurpassed.'

'What am I going to do? I have no access to what I care about most of all.'

'Be dignified, avoid showing your feelings, however unjustly you have been treated. I will inform Skoda.'

The following morning Josef Skoda, the recently appointed professor of medicine, waived aside Irma Valerie's protestations and strode into Klein's office.

'Ah, Professor Skoda,' Klein was not happy to see his unannounced visitor. 'I usually consult with colleagues by appointment but I am pleased to make an exception for our new illustrious professor of medicine.'

Skoda was not moved by Klein's obsequiousness. 'Professor Klein, you have dismissed Dr Semmelweis from his post as lecturer in your department?'

'Yes.'

115

'You gave no reason for this action?'

'Yes, I gave no reason, I did not have to, he is a meddlesome, interfering Hungarian who has worked against me.'

'You are a pompous, self serving idiot, Klein. You have succeeded in losing the services of a brilliant doctor and gaining a reputation for yourself of being monumentally stupid.'

Professor Josef Skoda could see that there was little point in prolonging the meeting. He turned and left.

There was no handshake, no acknowledgement for the dumbfounded head of the obstetric department of the Vienna General Hospital.

In that department the news of Semmelweis' departure spread like wildfire. Charlotte and her colleagues were devastated to learn that the doctor they most admired and relied upon had been dismissed from his post. Speculation was rife, and the wounded pride of people in high places still festered.

Furthermore, neither Skoda nor the staff of the obstetric department were aware that a commission had been established to investigate the alarmingly high mortality rate in the first obstetric clinic.

The three men who had been entrusted by the authorities to inquire into the matter were all from the Ministry of Public Education in Vienna. Only one was a doctor who had chosen administration as a career. He had been attracted to the free weekends and absence of night duties.

They had interviewed Klein in his office. 'To what, Professor, do you attribute the high death rates from childbed fever in the first obstetric clinic?' It was a lay member who had asked the question.

'My colleagues and I have examined this problem in great detail and have come to the conclusion it is due to the poor, damp conditions of the walls,' he lied confidently.

116

There had been no such 'examination' and he considered that it was the fate of these women to die.

Ignaz Semmelweis had also been approached by the same group who had asked him about the state of the walls. They had not mentioned the name of the departmental chief who had prompted the question.

'Gentlemen,' said Semmelweis, 'there are hospitals throughout Europe with far worse physical conditions than we have here. In many of them there is a very low incidence of childbed fever.'

'How do you know this?'

'Because I have written to all of them about this particular subject. Most of these hospital maternity departments had the courtesy to reply and gave the relevant information.'

'Do you believe them?'

'Yes, in some cases I have had independent corroboration from individual doctors who have visited Vienna.'

The commission preferred to trust the words of this young Hungarian doctor.

On 18 October 1846 Klein had received a chilling letter from the three wise men.

It was no coincidence that the dismissal of Semmelweis had taken place two days afterwards.

28

A Ray of Light

November 1846 had passed and Christmas was approaching. Vienna was becoming very cold and snow had started to fall.

Klein had extended Franz Breit's appointment by two years. This had given Semmelweis no hope of returning to his job in the first obstetric clinic.

He had written to numerous hospitals seeking work. Most did not reply, some said they had nothing available but one had given him a glimmer of optimism.

The Rotunda Maternity Hospital in Dublin was already gaining a reputation as a centre of excellence for its lying-in methods. The assistant clinical director had written back to Ignaz and expressed interest in him and his research.

Unfortunately Semmelweis had only managed to write the covering letter in stilted English and the remainder of his *curriculum vitae* had been in German. At the Rotunda they had taken the trouble to have the account of his work and ideas translated into English.

Therefore, the letter of reply concluded, 'We would like to see you here in Dublin in due course but we would urge you to improve your skills in English. We would be grateful if you would write to us again in six months time.'

118

Ignaz had hunted around the many bookshops of Vienna and eventually had found what he was searching for; *English As She Is Spoke* by Cavolino, published in Paris the previous year.

Opening the cover he read, 'A guide to conversation in English and Portuguese'. The irony of the title was lost on him. Anyway it was the only suitable volume he could lay his hands on.

Later that evening he was sitting in his apartment struggling with the first few pages of his purchase when Lajos Markusovszky came home.

'Hello there.' He was pleased to see his friend reading a book. Ignaz had been so depressed in recent days that even glancing at the *Vienna Medical Weekly* became a chore.

'Greetings.' There was a cheerfulness in his voice. 'I've had a letter from Ireland.' He handed the document, with the wax seal that he had broken, to Markusovsky.

'I'll take my coat off first, the snow on it is starting to melt.' He was delighted to see his friend in much better humour but he was also the bearer of good news.

He read the Irish doctor's letter. 'So that is why you are brushing up on your English?' He pointed to the book on the table with the easily readable title.

'It is, indeed,' a note of doubt crept into his voice. 'This language is difficult enough to read, let alone pronounce.' He was correct!

'You may not need it.'

'Need what?'

'The English.'

'Why?'

'Because, my good friend, the professorial chair in midwifery at Tübingen has become vacant.'

'They would never give that job to me.'

'Probably not, but they might appoint Franz Breit.' Lajos was cautious. 'I think he might apply for it.'

'I would never get back into the Vienna General Hospital.'

'Have a little belief in yourself.'

At that moment there was a soft tapping on the entrance door to the apartment. Markusovsky went to investigate.

'Is Doctor Ignaz Semmelweis at home?' It was a woman's voice.

'He certainly is, young lady.'

'My name is Charlotte Weiss. I am a midwife at the hospital.'

'Please, come in out of the cold.' Charlotte had been grateful for her only coat on her way to this apartment. It had been a long walk.

When she came into the small living room Semmelweis was already standing. 'Miss Weiss,' he gave a formal bow, 'how very nice to see you. I have missed your cheerful and kind professionalism since I left the obstetric clinic. Please let me take your coat and then sit down.' He indicated their third and last chair.

Seated but not relaxed Charlotte took a deep breath and began. 'Dr Semmelweis, I apologise for intruding into your home in the evening but it is the only off duty time I have at this moment.' He admired her new uniform but was alarmed at her obvious discomfort and embarrassment.

'Miss Weiss, or may I call you Charlotte?'

'Of course.'

'Be at ease, sit back and start at the beginning.'

'Thank you, Dr Semmelweis.' She was visibly less tense as she leant back in the chair. 'My midwife colleagues in both the first and second obstetric clinics have chosen me to visit you. Firstly, may I enquire if you are in good health?'

'That is most kind of you, Charlotte. Physically I am well, I have taught myself a little cookery in the past month and have to say I make a very fine boiled egg.'

'Man cannot live by eggs alone.' She smiled at her own misquotation.

'That is true but I do supplement them with daily visits to Miss Laura Drauz's coffee shop which is close by.' He smiled back at her.

'I think you have lost a little weight. I expect you to have regained it by the time I see you again.' She rose from her chair, went to her coat and removed a sizable parcel from the pocket in the lining.

'No wonder I thought that the coat was a bit on the heavy side,' Lajos grinned.

She placed her package on the small table. 'Veal pie, apples, bread rolls, butter and home-made plum jam.' She did not tell him that the food had been prepared by Edith. Collecting it from Maria Theresien Strasse had delayed her arrival.

'You are most kind, please give my grateful thanks to your colleagues.' Semmelweis was deeply touched by such concern for his welfare. His eyes were moist and a single tear rolled down his left cheek, which he rapidly brushed away.

'And your spirits?'

'I have to admit to some depression. However, I occupy my time writing letters searching for work.' Semmelweis was not ashamed to be honest.

'We want you back in the Vienna General Hospital,' Charlotte continued with a passionate sincerity. 'The maternity department has rapidly deteriorated, there is no hand washing, patients are treated rudely and roughly by the doctors and students, childbed fever is rife and morale is very low.'

'Your news saddens me.'

'It seems to us that the change in behaviour and practice of the medical staff is a result of orders from the top.' She had been hesitant about mentioning this last part.

'You refer to the professor?'

'I cannot say but we desperately need you.'

Lajos Markusovszky had listened carefully and since he worked in the surgical department knew little of these matters, although hospital gossip spoke of nothing else. 'I think Doctor Semmelweis will return.'

'What can we do to help that?'

'Nothing at present, except to practise his principles to the best of your abilities.'

'Thank you, both of you for your kindness, time and patience. I must leave, it is getting late.'

'It is we who should thank you,' said Lajos as he helped her on with her coat and opened the door for her. She went into the cold night a little happier.

29

Reinstated

Christmas 1846 passed and the New Year was heralded in Vienna by violent snowstorms. It was bitterly cold.

Lajos Markusovszky stayed in the apartment during the festive season although he could have returned to his family in Pest. He preferred to be with his colleague and comrade.

On 6 January 1847 Franz Breit was appointed professor of midwifery at Tübingen, the university town in the Baden province of south-west Germany.

On 10 January 1847 Doctor Ferdinand Von Hebra, head of the department of skin diseases, Professor Leopold Kolletschka, forensic pathologist, Professor Josef Skoda of internal thoracic medicine and Professor Karl Rokitanski, the pathological anatomist, were gathered around the table of the hospital boardroom with its chestnut-wood panelled walls.

A fifth chair was, as yet, unoccupied. There was no administrator present and especially no Irma Valerie. The four men were silent, each alone with his thoughts.

Markusovszky had approached Skoda with the news of Breit's new professorship and had bluntly told him, 'I don't think that there is a snowflake's chance in hell that Klein will let Doctor Semmelweis back into the obstetric unit. He regards Ignaz as a threat and indeed this is correct. I have watched him work at home; he has accumulated a vast amount of information very much suggesting that childbed fever is caused by doctors bringing contaminated material on their hands from the post-mortem room to the obstetric clinic.'

Skoda's eyebrows shot up in astonishment.

'Do they indeed? Are you quite sure?'

'Absolutely certain.'

'So, there is mischief afoot. We shall see what we have not seen before.'

The astute inventor of the stethoscope had spoken to his three colleagues and that was the reason why they were now sitting in silence.

Professor Johann Klein ambled into the room ten minutes late. He gave no greeting to the assembled senior doctors and sat down in the empty chair with a grunt. 'What do you lot want?'

Karl Rokitanski took the initiative. 'What we want, as you so delicately put it, is for you to reinstate Dr Semmelweis in his post as lecturer in your department.'

'Impossible.'

'Nothing is impossible for you, Professor, except perhaps courteousness,' Rokitanski's tone was ice cold.

'How often do you wash your hands?' Kolletschka's question was barbed.

'If you're talking about all that nonsense of Semmelweis', we know it's a fantasy. He had meddled and interfered in the first obstetric clinic for long enough, he had to go.'

'Don't you like Hungarian doctors?' Von Hebra looked quizzically at Klein and noticed he was sweating in January.

'That's nothing to do with it.'

'As you know, sir, I am the editor of the *Vienna Medical Weekly* and it is widely read throughout the Austro-Hungarian Empire.' Skoda was getting into his stride.

124

'Rumour has it that the journal is read in the royal palaces.'

'What if it is?' Klein shifted uneasily in his chair.

'I also have in my possession two interesting letters, one from Heidelberg and the other from Würzburg. I am quite prepared to publish them and an account of this meeting.'

Klein crumpled. He muttered, 'All right. I'll reinstate him from the first of April when Breit starts in Tübingen.'

'You will post notices to that effect throughout the hospital today?' Rokitanski was firm.

'Yes.'

Markusovszky was one of the first people to read the notice of Semmelweis' reinstatement. He hurried home as soon as his duties allowed.

On entering the apartment he was greeted by, 'He hung his hat on the hook in the hall of the Hungarian house.'

'What on God's earth are you talking about?'

'I am mastering the pronouncing of the English letter "aitch".' Ignaz grinned as he stood up and placed his remarkable 'Teach Yourself English Conversation' book on the sitting-room table. ' "Aitch" is a very difficult letter to articulate, you have to take a deep breath before you can do it.'

'You definitely won't need it.'

'What did you say?'

'You start work in the first obstetric clinic on April first. You've got your job back.' Lajos then told him of the notice posted up on boards throughout the hospital.

'This is not a joke to make me feel better?'

'No joke.'

Semmelweis sat down. 'I can't believe it.'

'It's true.'

'What am I going to do with myself for the next two months?'

'Ignaz, when you return to the hospital I believe you are going to introduce chlorine hand washing for all maternity students, doctors and nurses. Is that correct?'

'Yes.'

'You will have to prepare a reasoned and diplomatic thesis to facilitate such a change.'

'You are quite right.'

Markusovszky was smiling, 'Please keep it simple and try to limit it to one or two printed pages. My simple brain must be able to understand it.' He laughed. Markusovszky was certainly not stupid; in fact he was highly intelligent and articulate. He was to become a remarkable figure in the medical profession in Hungary in the nineteenth century. A pioneer of medical science.

Semmelweis was also smiling. 'I will do my best.'

'I know you will.' Changing the subject he went on, 'This has been a difficult year for you, relentless work and research followed by the disgraceful behaviour of Klein. You are physically and intellectually exhausted and I have to say all this has affected me.'

'Lajos, you have been a wonderful support.'

'Thank you. We both need a holiday.'

'I have been away from work too long.'

'You need a holiday, we both need a holiday.' Markusovszky was insistent. 'Where shall we go?'

'It is true. I need to refresh my depressed spirits that have been so very much tried by events at the clinic.'

'You do. Now where?'

'I have always wished to see Venice – the canals, bridges and wonderful art treasures.'

'Venice it is, you can use some of the next few weeks to plan the journey.'

'I always get the easy jobs,' they both roared with laughter and embraced in true friendship.

30

Half Day Off

It was the first Sunday in March 1847. Charlotte was at home in number ten Maria Theresien Strasse. She had managed to be relieved of her midwifery duties a little early on an unusually quiet day in the first obstetric clinic.

After a brisk walk she had arrived at the Orlov home just before one o'clock in the afternoon. Edith had prepared a wonderful lunch of venison from the Austrian countryside.

Alexandra, now nearly twenty-one months old, was toddling around the floor of the book-lined front room. She came to one of the legs of the chair on which Charlotte was sitting and used it to hold on to and tugged at her mother's skirt. She looked up and gave a beautiful smile revealing white teeth. A proud parent gently laid a hand on the child's head.

'That was a wonderful lunch, Charlotte,' said Rudolf from the chair opposite. 'It was made more so by having you with us, looking well and happy.' They were alone in the room apart from the midwife's daughter. 'Tell me about the hospital.'

'I love the work but we still have the terrible problem of childbed fever.'

'How many are affected?' Rudolf showed real concern and interest.

'Last month we lost forty-seven mothers and forty-two babies.'

'You mean the infants have the same disease?'

'Not exactly; I am told by the doctors that they have abscesses in the brain, lungs, liver and other organs at post-mortem examination, but the genitals are not affected.'

'That is amazing, Charlotte; I have to ask as a curious layman how the women's reproductive parts are afflicted?'

'There is awful swelling, discharge and even black dead bits with a terrible smell on the outside. The doctors say it is even worse on the inside.'

'How are your emotions when you see all of these dreadful things?'

'To start with I couldn't sleep at night thinking about the great suffering. I talked with Tutor Suzanne and she identifies with my feelings but said that until there is change we have to accept these things and relieve pain, fever and anxiety in whatever way we can.'

Rudolf seized on one word, 'Do you think there can be change?'

'I don't know.' Charlotte's face brightened. 'One thing is going to change. Dr Semmelweis is coming back to us.'

'That is good news. From what you told me over Christmas, his dismissal last October was completely unjust.'

'Oh, it was.' She nodded and picked up her daughter, sat her on her lap and hugged the fair-haired and blue-eyed little girl. 'Doctor Ignaz is a kind, gentle and brilliant maternity specialist.'

'What does he think about the deaths from childbed fever?' Rudolf's inquisition did not seem to upset Charlotte. Indeed she welcomed it.

'We, as midwives, all know and can see that he has dedicated his career to midwifery and is distressed like us by the agony of these poor women.'

'You admire him?'

'We all do. Not only does he do his clinical work but he studies autopsies of patients who have died of the fever and has been analysing the department's records since the hospital opened.'

'Is this just admiration?'

'What do you mean?'

'You seem to know so much about the man.'

'He is superb.'

'Are you in love with him?'

Charlotte was truly taken aback by this last question. She was silent for a few moments and then chose her words carefully. 'I love his attitude to suffering women. I love his humanity, but I do not presume to love him as a potential husband.'

Rudolf laughed. 'I apologise, I should never have asked you that. Please forgive me.'

'There is nothing to forgive.' She was also laughing.

'What do you think Dr Semmelweis might do when he returns to the clinic?'

'He had a small pilot scheme of chlorine hand washing for the foreign doctors who had been sent away because the authorities thought they caused childbed fever. It was shortly before he left.'

'Amazing prejudice! What happened?'

'None of the patients they examined got ill.' She frowned. 'I felt very badly about the way they were treated, I mean the foreign doctors.'

'You were right to do so.' Rudolf's voice showed his pride in his protégée.

'I and my colleagues think he may ask everybody to wash their hands.'

'Including the professor?'

'Him, too,' Charlotte giggled at the thought. At that moment the door burst open and in swept Georgina, Franz and Kate who jumped up on to her father's lap.

'Papa, Papa!' she proclaimed with excitement, 'we want to ask Charlotte a question.'

'Do you now?'

Franz answered for her, 'Yes we do and it's a very important one.'

'What have you three been plotting?'

'It's not a real plot, Papa,' Georgina chimed in. 'We think it's a beautiful idea.'

Charlotte put little Alexandra on the floor and she immediately ran unsteadily towards Franz. 'You see, young man, you are attracting the ladies already.' He blushed. 'I'm in suspense, please ask away.'

'Who is your spokesman, then?' the father asked the bubbling trio.

'Dearest Charlotte,' Georgina began, 'we are all very proud of you and love you and little Alexandra.' She paused for a moment. 'We also loved our mother and still love her even though we cannot see her.' It was getting difficult, she knew she had to get to the point. 'Could you – would you, marry Papa?'

Charlotte was astonished; Rudolf was deeply embarrassed.

It was the recently qualified young midwife who was able to find words to answer Georgina's eloquent speech.

'I have to thank you, all three of you. I am deeply moved by your lovely thoughts. I am especially pleased by what you said about your mother.' Rudolf and his children listened to her intently. 'Your father is a marvellous and kind man, he saw me at the lowest point in my life. I had no money, no home and no hope. I had a baby I loved but could not care for, I would have lost her to the foundling home and she too would have faced a bleak future. Rudolf Orlov rescued us.'

She knew that she could not stop here, 'From him I have gained a home, an education and a profession; I

130

have also kept my child. My gratitude to your father is so great that words are not enough nor–' she hesitated.

'Is marriage,' it was Edith who finished the sentence. She had silently and unobtrusively entered the room at the beginning of Georgina's unorthodox proposal.

'What you have said is appreciation enough. You and your daughter have enriched this house and brought even more happiness than we had when I first came here and that is saying a great deal.'

Rudolf Orlov felt he had to speak. 'My three angels, your thoughts about Charlotte have touched me greatly, but I must agree with Edith, I cannot marry her – ever. I have always thought that in this world where we live there is great suffering, poverty and injustice; to give coins to beggars or contributions to great projects was not right. I never do that and many don't like me as a result.'

No one moved, 'I believe it is better to help a single individual greatly than to try to cure all the ills of this planet. In the tragic moments when I saw Charlotte Weiss after the death of your dear mother I knew I had found that one person whom I wanted to help.'

Edith broke the spell. 'Come on, everybody, coats on and we will walk our talented midwife part of the way back to the hospital, as far as Karen Lindmeier's coffee shop.'

There was a rush to the door.

131

31

Venice

The railway engine, bright green with a tall, black smokestack idly puffing small plumes of grey haze was standing by the platform of Vienna Station. Four yellow and brown carriages were coupled behind it.

The terminal and northern network to Hungary and Germany had initially been in the private hands of F.A. Von Gertner and building had commenced in 1832. Known as the Kaiser Ferdinand line, it was taken over by the state ten years later. In 1846 it had introduced the first night service in Europe. Between 1839 and 1842 the southbound line to Gloggnitz had been completed. Its extension via Graz to Trieste was not finished until 1859 and was to be the first mountain railway on the continent.

By the time Semmelweis and Markusovszky boarded this train on 2 March 1847 they knew it would be necessary to transfer to a coach and horses some distance to the south of Graz for the journey on to the Adriatic sea port. This would be followed by taking one of the frequent ferries across to Venice.

A large cloud of black smoke emerged from the locomotive and with a barely perceptible jolt it pulled away from the city. Ignaz settled back in his seat as the modern wonder gathered speed. He watched, fascinated, as he saw the wealthier suburbs of Vienna pass by and shortly afterwards the vast tenement area occupied by the poor, the unemployed and the flotsam found in every large metropolis. Suddenly the green fields of the flat countryside appeared. In the far distance the faint outline of the Austrian Tyrol could be seen in the south-west.

'We should have done this months ago, Lajos.'

'You're right, I feel invigorated already.'

'That was quick.'

'I am very sensitive to my environment.'

The two men arrived in Venice the following afternoon and soon found the comfortable Hotel Monaco, with two adjacent rooms overlooking the Grand Canal.

Ignaz had, in his characteristic meticulous way, prepared a list of the buildings and treasures he wished to see.

He showed it to his fellow tourist. 'Goodness gracious me, is there anything you don't want to see?'

'Not much.'

'How did you find out about all these things?'

'You told me to organise the travelling arrangements, so I thought it would be a good idea to decide what we were going to do when we arrived.'

Lajos had visions of Semmelweis surrounded by the records of the obstetric department of the Vienna General Hospital, but this time it was art and travel books of Venice.

Both of them had been able to save some money in Vienna from their pitiful salaries but these were greatly supplemented by giving private tutorials to the more wealthy students. Their lifestyles were frugal with little socialising due to the arduous work schedule.

They had a wonderful meal in the hotel and the luxury of an early night to recover from the trip and prepare for the next day's activities.

Refreshed and enthusiastic they stepped out the following morning into bright sunshine and a light breeze. 'Let's take it gently, Ignaz. We have plenty of time and I don't want to suffer from cultural indigestion. Where first?'

'It has to be the Piazza and Basilica of San Marco and if we have time the Doge's Palace. Doge means Duke, you know. He and his successors ruled Venice from 697 until 1797.' Semmelweis' enthusiasm was infectious.

Markusovszky hailed one of the many black gondolas plying for trade on the Grand Canal. While they waited for it to come over to them he said, 'Have you noticed quite a number of foreigners are here?'

'Mostly English, I think.'

'They've got pretty expensive clothes.'

'It's part of what the upper classes call their grand tour. The great and the good go to all the fashionable parts of Europe such as Paris, Biarritz and Naples.'

'Sounds to me more like the rich and idle classes.' They both laughed and stepped into the small boat and sat on one of the red velvet cushioned benches.

As they glided along the water Ignaz began to give his friend a brief history of Venice. 'The Doges ruled from 697 to 1797, when Napoleon surrendered it to our glorious Hapsburgs.' These last two words were uttered tongue in cheek. In fact he was attracted to the revolutionary talk that was quietly taking place in the coffee shops of Vienna.

'As ever, you have done your homework.'

'I had the time,' Semmelweis smiled. 'Greater Venice stands on one hundred and eighteen islets and the city itself is criss-crossed by one hundred and sixty canals, with over six hundred bridges.'

'Your statistics are showing again.'

'Thank you. Our hotel stands only one metre above sea level, therefore the ground floor is used as a basement for storage and sometimes gets flooded. Most of the newer buildings in Venice are the same; the walls are open with boats moored to the supports.'

Semmelweis was enjoying himself. 'Marco Polo set out from here at the age of seventeen in 1271 and was away for twenty-five years. He passed through Baghdad, Persia, Afghanistan and eventually arrived at the court of Prince Kublai Khan, the ruler of Mongolia.'

'A long holiday.'

'A very, very long holiday. He opened up trade with the east and Venice prospered – and how she prospered. In the sixteenth century Titian and Tintoretto worked here and with wealth came power. It had a great army resisting the Turks and Hapsburgs, but in the eighteenth century it degenerated a little, with the writings of Giacomo Casanova and widespread gambling. Now it is under the rule of Austria.'

Their water transport came to a halt, they paid the gondolier, alighted and soon made their way to the Piazza San Marco and its richly decorated and multi-domed Basilica. 'Amazing,' said Ignaz. 'Legend has it that the Venetians stole the relics of Saint Mark from Alexandria in 828, and here we see the influence of Byzantium, which must be the result of that great expedition by Marco Polo.'

'You're a fount of knowledge, Ignaz, but you're right, this is an astounding sight.' They made their way through the few other tourists who were there in March, to the centre of the Piazza and stopped to look at their surroundings. On three sides were three tiered arcades with shops on the ground level and at the east end stood the Basilica with the Doge's Palace extending from its south walls. 'Let us enter.'

They spent the whole day there, marvelling at the mosaics on the walls glinting with gold and depicting scenes of the life of Christ, the kiss of Judas and many saints. Lajos admired the columns and domed ceilings. Ignaz pointed out the tranquil ambience.

When the two doctors emerged from one of the four bronze doors, the sun was already setting, casting huge shadows across the Piazza.

'The Doge will have to wait until tomorrow.'

'I agree. Anyway I'm hungry.'

'Hungry? I think it's the first time I have heard you use that word, Ignaz.'

'I do eat, you know,' he answered as they stepped on to a waiting gondola. That evening their supper was a delicious fish risotto.

They returned to the Doge's Palace the next day. Its breathtaking interior starting with the golden staircase and finishing in the *Sala dello Scrutinio*, with its mosaic of the last judgement, left them almost speechless.

Again a full day was occupied. They came out to rain but it was a short shower.

'What went on in that last room, Ignaz?'

'It was used to count the votes of the Doge's council.'

'Incredible.'

The time passed quickly; they saw all they could of this treasure of a city. Markusovszky noted Semmelweis' mood was greatly improved, he was eating well, had put on a little weight and frequently smiled.

By 20 March 1847 the pair had made the return journey to Vienna. On arrival they discovered that Professor Jakob Kolletschka was dead.

32

Kolletschka's Death

Although he was not officially due to take up his assistant lecturer post until 1 April, Semmelweis did, in fact, resume his duties on 22 March 1847.

En route to the first obstetric clinic he visited the widow of his mentor and friend Jakob Kolletschka. He brought with him a beautiful blue and white flower vase, which he had bought in the Murano glass factory during his time in Venice. In it he had placed a single white rose.

'Please accept my sincere condolences and this small gift in memory of your husband. He was a great man and good friend to me.'

The woman, dressed entirely in black, took the offering in both her hands. 'Thank you, Doctor Semmelweis,' a tear rolled down her left cheek. 'I did miss you at the funeral, but knew you were away on a well-earned holiday.'

'I am so very sorry, if there is anything I can do for you, please do not hesitate to ask.'

'There is one thing. Jakob liked, admired and trusted you. Would you be kind enough to look at his medical and autopsy reports? I would value your opinion.'

'It will be an honour and a duty that I shall undertake as soon as possible.' He gave the elegant but sad lady a formal bow and departed.

On entering the main lying-in ward of the clinic he was

struck by the awful smell of dead and rotting human flesh. Childbed fever was rampant. He was greeted enthusiastically by doctors, midwives, students and some puerperal women. There was polite applause in which Charlotte took part. Klein and Irma Valerie were not present.

The handshaking and welcoming completed he was conducted around all the patients. A bowl of warm water, soap and bristle nailbrush together with clean towels were already standing beside the first bed.

He moved round unhurriedly, stopping and washing his hands at every bed, mostly listening, sometimes asking a question and always speaking gently to the fearful women.

At the end of his tour he briefly discussed chlorine hand washing and his two-page paper that had been printed. He said he would distribute it after seeking permission from the professor. He then hurried off to find the records of Kolletschka's illness and post-mortem examination.

The clinical account had been remarkably well documented in a clear, stylish hand. He guessed this had been written by a medical student in the surgical department. It was followed by the admitting doctor's notes, which were brief and hurriedly written. It transpired that Kolletschka, who frequently had the assistance of a medical student when performing forensic autopsies, was dissecting the putrid corpse of a poor wretch who had been pulled out of the Danube during the last week in February.

The nervous student accidentally let his post-mortem knife slip and it had penetrated one of the professor's fingers. Within twenty-four hours the lacerated skin had become painful, swollen and dark red with blue-black areas. The disease rapidly spread to the veins and lymph vessels in his arm, followed by the development of enlarged painful lymphatic glands in the axilla of the same side.

138

He was admitted to the surgical department with a diagnosis of phlebitis and lymphangitis.

Poultices were applied, laudanum was given and an incision made in the axillary swellings. He did not improve and developed chest pain, shortness of breath and vomiting. The doctors found a high fever, tenderness in a distended abdomen and frank suppurating gangrene spreading up the affected arm. He died on 4 March 1847, two days after Semmelweis left for Venice. Shortly before death a massive swelling had developed in his left eye; there had been great pain and blindness.

The autopsy findings showed pleurisy, pericarditis, peritonitis and multiple metastatic abcesses, including one in the left eye.

Semmelweis made notes from the file and then returned it to the archives. As he walked to his apartment his mind was in turmoil. He had already been in an excited state after seeing the marvels of Venice, but all that was now quickly put out of his mind. He visualised poor Kolletschka lying, cut open in the post-mortem room. The thick foul-smelling fluid in the chest cavity; it even surrounded the heart inside its covering membrane, the pericardium. The same changes were in the peritoneal cavity with loops of intestine stuck together by gelatinous material and abcesses in many parts of the body, including that awful eye. Apart from there being no uterus and its attachments these were exactly the same changes he had seen in so many women who died of childbed fever.

It was not the knife that killed Kolletschka, but the particles of dead decaying matter on it that had been introduced into his bloodstream. He had to ask himself, could the same process happen in childbed fever? And he had to answer himself, yes.

A little later he was in the apartment explaining his discovery and thoughts to Markusovszky. 'You see Lajos, cadaveric particles can be carried on doctor's hands from the autopsies and introduced into the circulating blood of some women through their bruised and lacerated birth canal.' A frown and then a look of horror changed his expression, 'I must have done it a thousand times myself.'

'Don't reproach yourself so much, it is still an hypothesis.'

Ignaz's thoughts raced ahead. 'Lajos, after performing an autopsy there is a dreadful smell on the hands. It is not removed by scrubbing with soap and water but it is removed by a solution of chlorinated lime. That smell must be due to cadaveric particles that are only destroyed by the chemical.'

'I think you have something there, my friend, but there is a great deal of work ahead – and opposition.'

'And opposition,' repeated Semmelweis.

What an understatement that proved to be!

33

Chlorine Hand Washing

Semmelweis knocked on the door of Professor Johan Klein's office. He had thought of bringing a colleague for support but had decided this was a battle he had to fight alone.

'Come in.'

He entered the plush room and found Irma Valerie seated beside the head of the obstetric department. Neither rose to greet him. 'Why are you here?'

'Professor, I have the honour to present, for your approval, my case for introducing chlorine hand washing in the first and second obstetric clinics of the Vienna General Hospital.' He handed the two printed sheets to Klein. He was not offered a chair.

'You are treading on thin ice, doctor,' Irma Valerie glowered at the Hungarian.

The professor ignored her; he had clear recollections of his recent interview with Rokitanski, Skoda, Von Hebra and the late Kolletschka. 'What is *chlorina liquida*?'

'It is water that has had chlorine gas bubbled through it – very expensive, but chloride of lime is equally effective, cheap and we could order some, with your approval.'

Klein continued reading through to the end. There was a tangible silence. Irma Valerie looked enquiringly with raised eyebrows at her idol. He scribbled on a piece of

141

paper and handed it to Semmelweis. 'You have my permission, that is all.'

While closing the door behind him, Ignaz heard, 'Do not worry yourself, Irma, this is the whim of an over-ambitious Hungarian. New facts will contradict our Doctor Semmelweis.'

'Oh will they?' Semmelweis whispered to himself as he made his way to the hospital supplies office and its chief official.

'You want what?' Horst Vomberg's already rubicund features turned purple and his neck veins stood out. He had not got up from his chair behind a desk stacked with invoices, final demands for payment and broken surgical instruments.

Ignaz again waved Klein's scrappy piece of paper in his round face, 'All your *chlorina liquida*, twenty new porcelain washbowls and water jugs; four mobile washstands on well oiled wheels and one hundred new hand towels.'

'That is ridiculous. Anyway, *chlorina liquida* is very expensive.'

'That is why you will immediately place an order for chlorinated lime.' Then almost as an afterthought, 'I believe your good wife is due to give birth next month.'

Resistance crumbled. 'All this to be delivered to the midwifery clinics before the end of April?'

'Exactly,' smiled Semmelweis.

'I'll do my best.' Poor Horst, he was afraid of Klein but terrified of his wife discovering any deficiency that may have been caused by him.

'Progress,' the young Hungarian said to no one in particular, as he climbed the three steps into Rokitanski's Institute of Pathology. He sought out Dr Lautner who was pioneering the use of animals in pathological studies.

He explained his theory on the cause of childbed fever.

142

'Do you think that there is any experimental way to support my hypothesis?'

Lautner belonged to the emerging group of medical scientists that were yet to be recognised in the world of the healing art. 'I suppose we could introduce decaying organic matter from women who have died of childbed fever into the vagina of an animal just after it has cast a litter. The rabbit is probably best.'

One week later fifty rabbits had been subjected to Lautner's suggested investigation. Forty-eight hours later seventy per cent were dead and at post-mortem examination they had the same changes as the dead women from whom the material had been extracted.

Semmelweis had mixed feelings that evening as he sat in the apartment with Markusovszky. 'Of course I'm pleased with the results, but I'm full of remorse at what I must have done to so many women.'

'You are far from being the only doctor in this situation. The difference is you are the only doctor here who has any insight into what may have happened.'

'I thank you for that but how can I begin to help these dead women?'

'You already are,' Lajos leaned forward. 'My very good friend, you must publish. Perhaps make a start with the rabbit experiment.'

'I will talk to Dr Lautner.'

During the first week of April new supplies began to arrive in Professor Klein's department.

At eight o'clock in the morning of 1 May 1847 chlorine hand washing became compulsory in the first and second obstetric clinics of the Vienna General Hospital.

34

Teaching the Technique

On this May day, Vienna was bathed in warm sunshine. Semmelweis arrived at the first obstetric clinic with a heart full of hope, enthusiasm and above all a burning belief that he could relieve the terrible suffering of childbed fever.

He had not made his usual early visit to the autopsy room, preferring instead to spend the time organising his thoughts in his mind. He had, on the previous day, asked two students to take his place and assist at a post-mortem examination on a fever victim before they came to the clinic that morning. An Austrian student, Werner Schmidt and a Hungarian, Janos Tibor had been deliberately selected. Ignaz was only too well aware of the prejudices that were rampant in the city.

He entered the lying-in room followed by Charlotte and another midwife pushing two bowls on mobile stands. Two more carried porcelain jugs and the little procession was completed by a pair who could barely see over the pile of clean towels they were carrying.

A group of doctors, medical students, midwives and nursing assistants awaited them; their chatter ceased when the lecturer appeared. The Professor, Irma Valerie and some students had failed to appear. All had been given the introductory pamphlet.

'Good morning ladies and gentlemen. We will begin today with a little demonstration using our olfactory apparatus.'

'Our what?' whispered a student.

'Our noses, you idiot,' his neighbour nudged him.

Ignaz was well aware of the pervading odour characteristic of childbed fever that struck anyone coming into the room. Equally the background sounds of suffering women seemed to be ever present. 'Mr Schmidt and Mr Tibor, would you kindly step forward?'

The two moved to the front of the group. 'Mr Schmidt can you tell everyone here what you did before you came to the clinic today?'

'I assisted Dr Wolfgang Freimuth in performing a post-mortem on a woman who died of childbed fever yesterday.'

'And you, Mr Tibor?'

'I assisted at the same autopsy.'

'Can you briefly tell us the findings?'

The student hesitated and looked enquiringly at the midwives who nodded encouragingly at him. 'There were abscesses in the lungs and liver, the uterus was enlarged and had loops of small intestine adherent to it, surrounded by thick, brown, foul-smelling fluid.'

'Did any of this material get on your hands or clothes?'

'Yes,' the two answered in unison.

'Then what did you do?'

'We washed our hands under the cold tap in the post-mortem room,' Tibor said.

'With soap?'

'There wasn't any there.'

'Do you think your hands still smell of that decaying organic material?'

'Yes,' replied the duo.

'Ladies and gentlemen, would you all kindly smell these young men's hands.'

Charlotte and her midwife colleagues smelt one pair of outstretched palms. Some noses wrinkled, and the men put the other offering to the test.

'Now, if you two young men would kindly take off your coats and roll up your shirtsleeves above the elbows.' The two obliged.

'Water, please.'

Charlotte and her colleagues pushed forward one of the bowls, filled it with steaming water from a jug, produced soap, a bristle nail brush and placed a towel on the lower rail of the washstand.

The two young men scrubbed and washed vigorously. Dried and without being asked they held out their hands for the collective nasal approval. The smell was still there, slightly reduced, but still present.

'Now we will put in the other bowl *chlorina liquida*, but gentlemen, a little less with the brush or there will be no skin left to admire.'

The two washed again. As they did so a fresh and pleasing odour came from their direction. Their hands dried they smelt the result for themselves, smiled and then stretched them out to the fascinated assembly which eagerly assessed the result.

'Amazing, isn't it?' said Semmelweis. 'From today it is washing before and after examining each of our women in the lying-in rooms. Are there any questions?'

An astonished Tibor enquired, 'How does it work?'

'In some way the chlorine destroys decaying organic matter. Let us proceed.' The ensuing ward round was necessarily slow but appreciated by all present, both staff and patients.

Semmelweis did not forget the obstetric element and his duty to teach. Between cases he spoke of examining the placenta or afterbirth to ensure it was complete; a detail relative to students and midwives alike.

Eventually the round finished and Charlotte held open the door for the Hungarian doctor. She smiled and whispered, 'Thank you – again.'

Ignaz was pleased with the morning's work but as he walked towards the nearest coffee shop he turned over in his mind the pathologic findings in dead mothers, infants and his mentor Professor Kolletschka. Perhaps childbed fever was not a single disease.

Of course, not all the relevant people had been present on that sunny first day of May. However, during the course of the month the chlorine hand washing became routine throughout the department. Even the great Professor Johann Klein accepted the ritual when it was first offered on his next Grand Round. Irma Valerie looked on contemptuously.

In the second clinic Tutor Suzanne supervised the process meticulously. Towards the middle of the month she had reason to visit Charlotte in the first clinic and was astounded at the change. 'That awful, putrid smell – it has not gone completely but it is very much less intense.'

'We have all noticed and so have the mothers.'

When Semmelweis collected the figures for the number of deaths from childbed fever in the first clinic for May he was disappointed to find it was thirty-two but in June the number was only five out of over 300 deliveries.

Now this was change, and for the first time both clinics were doing equally well.

35

Sabotage

In mid-July Charlotte with Alexandra, now two years old, and Edith had walked west from the Orlov house to the area of parkland near the university. Progress had been slow; the little girl sometimes asked to be carried and then to be put down to walk again holding her mother's hand.

Eventually they sat on the grass in the shade of a tree, while Alexandra inspected little flowers. Many others around them enjoyed this summer Sunday afternoon. 'Now where were we, Charlotte?'

'You really want to talk hospitals on a day like today, Edith?'

'I do indeed, every detail.'

'The *chlorina liquida* soon ran out of stock but miraculously vast quantities of chloride of lime had been ordered. It smells much nicer and doesn't irritate our hands.'

'What do the other midwives think about all this and your Dr Semmelweis?'

'He's not mine, Edith,' Charlotte smiled. 'My friends think he is wonderful, but he is very modest about his work.'

'That can only be a good thing; we live in a wicked world. If he really has changed the field of midwifery there are bound to be people in high places with vested interests who will try to destroy him.'

'Edith, it's happening already.'

'How do you know?'

'I found a student trying to avoid hand washing. He made a show of it but did not even get his hands wet.'

'What did you do?'

'It was difficult, he was Austrian and I did not want to be rude. Mr Gunther Hahn, I said, chlorine hand washing is usually a moist process and the towel will be greatly disappointed if it encounters dry hands and arms.'

'Humour always helps in these situations. You have learned wisdom and diplomacy, as well as midwifery – I congratulate this new Charlotte. What did he do?'

'He blushed profusely, then he smiled, rolled up his shirtsleeves higher still above his elbows and returned to the bowl. There was much splashing and scrubbing; after he was dry he offered me his hands to inspect and smell. We laughed together.'

'A triumph of brain over brawn, but that could hardly be part of a conspiracy?'

'No, I don't think it was, but what Tutor Suzanne experienced definitely was sinister.'

'What was that?'

'A doctor was called to the second clinic when a midwife thought that a labouring woman who had been pushing for two hours with the baby's head visible low down was too exhausted to give any more effort. She felt the forceps were indicated. Dr Von Humboldt is new, he did not take off his coat and went to pick up the forceps without giving the bowl of chloride of lime solution a glance.'

'Ah ha! Trouble.'

'Yes. The midwife pushed the bowl towards him and offered to hold his coat while he washed. He told her it was not necessary. Tutor Suzanne was passing and very firmly explained the new routine with a demonstration. He complied immediately and the child was delivered.'

149

'Was that all?' Edith was frowning.

'No. He was a very polite although formal young man. He walked with Tutor Suzanne to the door of the lying-in room and apologised. He then told her that after his interview with Klein for the junior post he had been seen out of the office by Irma Valerie, and she had told him not to be bothered by the silly hand washing that was going on.'

'Now that is sinister.' Edith let very little anger her but showed some venom on this occasion. 'That woman should have her wings clipped, preferably with a guillotine.'

Charlotte giggled. 'I would volunteer to work the machine.'

'That's not very ladylike. Has anything else happened that might damage Dr Semmelweis?'

'It's mostly gossip, but it's hurtful. Some have imitated his Hungarian accent, others say that he's all work and no play and there are a few doctors seething with jealousy.'

'How does Dr Semmelweis react to all this?'

'He remains the same, dignified, polite kind, respectful and very thoughtful. I think his holiday in Venice with Dr Markusovszky gave him renewed strength which puts him above all the pettiness.'

'You are probably right, Charlotte, but I think his biggest danger at the moment is Irma Valerie. Others may appear later.'

At that moment Alexandra trotted over to them with a new friend, an earthworm wriggling on her outstretched hand. The serious mood was broken and Charlotte helped her daughter gently put the worm back with his brothers and sisters.

'Time to go home,' Edith stood up. 'I know Rudolf and the rest of the family will want to see you before you go back to the hospital.'

As the trio slowly made their way home Charlotte asked Edith, 'Were they upset?'

150

'By what?'

'The marriage thing.'

'Oh no. Rudolf still loves his Alexandra and nothing will change that. Those three young people are so pleased to have you as part of the family and don't want to lose you.'

'And the question about Dr Semmelweis?'

'He was testing your professionalism and got the answer he expected.'

The door opened as mother, daughter and Edith mounted the steps of number ten.

36

Setback

The summer of 1847 was a very good one for the mothers and babies of both the obstetric clinics of the Vienna General Hospital. Childbed fever was at the low levels that had existed before 1822 and the morale of the midwives, students and doctors was high. Ignaz Semmelweis' confidence was cautiously growing.

Other departments were busy and beds fully occupied. Towards the end of September the gynaecology ward asked the first clinic to take in a terminally ill lady with cancer of the uterus. She was placed in bed number one where ward rounds began. Her tumour was fungating into the vagina and there was blood loss together with foul discharge.

A week later a woman with an ulcerated carious left knee joint was transferred from the surgical ward to bed number two. We now know that this condition was due to tuberculosis.

These two unfortunate women had not recently given birth and therefore chlorine hand washing was not required in their care or when teaching on those diseases took place.

On 5 October the woman in bed number three who had required a forceps delivery developed a fever, abdominal pain and a foul vaginal discharge. Charlotte was on duty and sent for Dr Semmelweis. 'She was really well this morning, doctor, but has become so very ill this afternoon.'

The lecturer took off his coat, rolled up his sleeves, washed in chloride of lime and examined the distressed woman. She was pale, sweating, had a rapid thready pulse and looked at him anxiously.

'I've got the fever, haven't I?' she asked breathlessly. 'Oh! oh! stop!' she shouted, as Semmelweis gently laid a hand on her already bloated belly. He did not proceed to palpate internally, there was no need, a foul discharge was staining the front of her thighs. 'Please drink this,' he handed her a cup of water, 'do not be alarmed and concentrate on the drinking.' His worst fears were confirmed.

He and the alert midwife moved away from the bed. 'Has there been any breach in the chlorine hand washing?'

'No doctor.'

'Tell me about these ladies in the first two beds. Do they have any fever?'

'No,' Charlotte explained why they were there.

Semmelweis drew back the blankets on the unfortunate cancer victim; she was comatose and a cadaveric odour was present. He inspected the second woman. Her left leg was swathed in bandages but a dark discolouring was present over the knee joint. He leant down and noticed the same unpleasant stench.

'There is something terribly wrong here. I do not know what it is but I do know it's wrong. Please keep me informed.' He left deep in thought.

In the evening the cancer patient passed away peacefully under the influence of laudanum. Early in the morning of the 6 October the poor woman in the third bed died in agony. Over the next two days the occupants of beds four to six were diagnosed as suffering from childbed fever. Curiously, the last two in beds five and six were mild and they recovered; the mother nearest to the disaster area succumbed.

The crippled lady whose knee ensured she would never walk again was taken back by the surgical ward during this tragic period.

Semmelweis had been badly shaken and talked to Markusovszky in their apartment. 'You see, Lajos, in some way ichorous particles must have been transferred from those two poor women to the lying-in mothers.'

'Ichorous, that is a new word to me.'

'I apologise, it just seemed the best word to describe that watery fetid discharge we see in women with tumours of the uterus. I suppose cadaveric would be better.'

'Where did you find such a strange term?'

Ignaz blushed, 'Poetry.'

'You don't read poetry.'

'I know, but my mother loved it. She used to read out loud to me, my brothers and sisters. I was only six years old when we listened to her recite, "Vision of Judgement" by Lord Byron. I had no idea what it meant but two lines became fixed in my mind.

Of course his perspiration was but ichor
or some such other spiritual liquor.'

'I'm impressed, but I think you should use conventional medical language otherwise Klein really will have ammunition to use against you.'

'Of course, you're right; it was a silly and pretentious thing to say. The point is, Lajos, if decaying organic matter from sick people who do not have childbed fever can cause the condition then it is not a single disease.'

Markusovszky took a few minutes to go over this statement in his mind.

'This would be an entirely new concept and very difficult to promote.'

'I know.'

154

'Perhaps you should go back to George Lautner and his rabbits. Ignaz, you will need scientific evidence and this time the material you put in the animals should be from other diseases that produce decaying organic matter, such as gangrenous limbs.'

'It certainly needs thinking about.'

'Ignaz, there is something I must tell. My time in the surgical department is coming to an end and I have decided to return to Pest.'

Semmelweis' face said it all. 'Lajos, you have been more than a friend – I shall miss you terribly. You were there when I was at my lowest ebb, you have buoyed me up and kept me going when I was so dispirited.'

Markusovszky put both hands on Semmelweis' shoulders and looked him in the eyes. 'You have, I believe, made a great discovery and the effect on mothers and babies in maternity hospitals throughout Europe will be dramatic.'

'I thank you for that and I wish you well in Pest. As for myself I have a strong belief that the truth about the concept, cause and prevention of childbed fever will come out.'

November 1847 saw only one death from childbed fever in the first obstetric clinic.

37

The Power of Print

The *Journal of the Medical Society of Vienna* was circulated to all the medical libraries of the universities of Europe and beyond. The December 1847 edition was dominated by its leading article submitted by Ferdinand Von Hebra and entitled 'Experience of the Highest Importance Concerning the Aetiology of Puerperal Fever, Prevalent at Lying-in Hospitals.'

He then proceeded to name Semmelweis, give an account of his observations, describe chlorine hand washing and report the dramatic fall in incidence of childbed fever. He concluded by inviting observations from other European maternity institutions.

The year drew to an end, Markusovszky left for Pest and on 31 December Ignaz answered a knock on the door of his small apartment. A tall slim man wearing a black coat and high bowler hat was standing in front of him.

'Good evening, Dr Semmelweis. My name is Rudolf Orlov. You may not remember me but I shall always be grateful for your kindness when my dear wife, Alexandra, died of transverse lie two and a half years ago.'

Recognition showed on Semmelweis' face, 'I do remember you. Please come in and sit down.' He took the coat and hat. 'It was you who took Miss Weiss and her child into your home. She has become one of our best midwives.'

'I am gladdened to hear you say that. She has brought light into our house and I believe has now dedicated her life to her profession.'

'She is a credit to our hospital and the lying-in women think she is an angel. She has also been of great assistance and support to me.' It was in Semmelweis' nature to speak well of people when it was merited.

'She admires your work, gentleness and humanity,' Rudolf pointed to the journal lying on the table. 'She brought that editorial home for me to read. I must congratulate you.'

'Thank you.'

'Charlotte tells me that your good friend and colleague Dr Markusovszky has returned to Pest. I am not a doctor but I do understand the ways of the world and I have come to tell you that if at any time you wish to talk to me, you will be most welcome.'

'Thank you again.'

'Dr Semmelweis, I wish you most sincerely every good fortune in 1848.' The men shook hands. Orlov left without further ado.

During the second week in January Dr Von Hebra sought out Ignaz in the first obstetric clinic. 'Ignaz, I would like to bring some visitors to your ward round next Thursday.'

'Ferdinand, I would be honoured. As you know my rounds are always open to interested doctors.'

At nine o'clock on the morning of 19 January 1848 Semmelweis, junior doctors, midwives and students were assembled in the lying-in ward of the first obstetric clinic. The door opened. Von Hebra held it to allow Rokitanski, Skoda and three other men to come into the room.

The waiting group were quietly amazed to see the visitors. 'Professors Rokitanski and Skoda are well known to you all,' Von Hebra was enthusiastic. 'May I introduce

157

Professor Gustav Michaelis of Kiel University, Professor Christian Tilanus from Amsterdam and Dr Jacob Sonderegger who is visiting us from Switzerland.'

The distinguished guests were known to Ignaz, at least in writing. He had written to the two professors asking about their experience of childbed fever and they had replied courteously. The Swiss physician was, he thought, the first doctor to have published a paper about hygiene in hospitals.

'Welcome gentlemen,' handshakes were exchanged. 'We will proceed in our routine fashion including chlorine hand washing, but please feel free to ask questions at any time.'

The visitors were kind and thoughtful to the lying-in women with, 'Good morning, how is your baby progressing?' and 'How do you find the experience of being in the obstetric clinic?'

'One woman had the courage to reply, 'This place used to have a terrible reputation. Many thought they would die but Dr Semmelweis has brought about a great change, we love him.'

Semmelweis blushed.

Rokitanski spoke for him. 'Dr Semmelweis has saved the lives of countless numbers of mothers and infants as a result of clinical observations, analysing the records of this hospital and others throughout Europe, and made a hypothesis. He has acted in a practical way as soon as he was able to do so and I am convinced he is right.'

Here was the most respected man in the Vienna General Hospital giving a resounding endorsement of Ignaz' work in the realistic surroundings of patients, nurses and doctors of all levels. He continued, 'I myself have subscribed for many years to the crasis theory of childbed fever – that is to say a primary disturbance of the blood. However, from today I am abandoning that teaching. Although it is true that the blood is affected, which accounts for the widespread manifestations of the disease found at autopsy, I now accept that it is secondary to the introduction of decaying organic material into the blood via the bruised and sometimes lacerated birth canal.' While he was speaking Irma Valerie had slipped into the room, unheard and unnoticed. Her face registered fury and contempt. She said nothing.

The Swiss doctor asked about the composition of the chloride of lime solution. Semmelweis smiled, 'I am no chemist but my pharmacological colleagues tell me it is *chlor. calcis unc.* 1 part and *aqua fontanae libras duas.*'

The visitors were making notes.

The round drew to its conclusion and the visitors expressed their gratitude. Professor Tilanus spoke for the first time. 'Dr Semmelweis, you have given us a wonderful demonstration backed by powerful arguments for the cause and prevention of childbed fever, and I shall certainly be introducing your methods. However, I wonder if you have completely ruled out atmospheric influences?'

'No. It would seem to me that if the air was heavy with moisture in a confined space where there is a large number of women with childbed fever, such droplets could be carried to the injured genitals of women who have just given birth. However, I believe such circumstances are now rare here in Vienna.'

Professor Michaelis was silent and there was a forlorn expression on his face.

38

Riots

The sun was indeed shining on the obstetric department of the Vienna General Hospital in the early weeks of 1848. However, it neglected to even glimmer on Professor Johann Klein who was cast into a shadow of severely dented vanity and seething jealousy.

He was rarely seen around his own domain and his dark mood blackened when Irma Valerie reported what she had seen and heard on Semmelweis' ward round.

'Professor, these people, important visitors come here to see that Hungarian upstart. They ignore you and your name is not even mentioned.'

'What do you know about our lecturer's political connections?'

'Nothing, but I can easily believe he is an anarchist.'

'We had better see what we can find out then.'

'Yes, Professor.' Irma Valerie smiled as she left his office. Klein was also smiling as the door closed behind her.

The head of the obstetric department may have been a prejudiced bigot but he was not a fool. As far as he was concerned childbed fever was a quirk of fate mediated by the atmosphere. It was his teaching and that was that. Why should he care if a few poor women died; what did matter was that this obnoxious little Hungarian was a threat to his position, his power and his standing in the eyes of the rich members of the imperial court.

His evenings at the dinner tables of the nobility gave him insight into the impending unrest in Vienna: a welcome diversion, a smokescreen that would soon stop the chatter about chlorine hand washing.

He knew that the essentially rural economy of the Austro-Hungarian Empire had, for a long time, been undermined by the feudal labour and land tax, called *robot*. Over the past thirty years it had driven many of the agricultural population to the cities and Vienna was now swelled to 400,000 people. He was well aware that this was a source of cheap industrial labour, but there was no industrial revolution. There were none of the chimneys of the Ruhr because there was no coal. Instead there was unemployment and poverty.

There were similar events in Hungary and northern Italy, ruled over by the unstable Hapsburg dynasty, which for as long as most people could remember had been dominated by Metternich, the foreign minister.

Unrest in the city was palpable and the poor were urged on mostly by students, the future bureaucracy. This was the intellectual stimulus, with the notable exception of medical undergraduates. Nevertheless, reasoned Klein, if Semmelweis could be shown to be involved it would finish him.

On 13 March 1848 riots broke out in the streets of Vienna. Among the compromises that followed was the fall of Metternich; among the injured lay Irma Valerie, barely conscious when admitted to the surgical ward of the Vienna General Hospital.

During this upheaval Semmelweis received letters from Professors Tilanus and Michaelis reporting dramatic falls in the occurrence of childbed fever following the introduction of chlorine hand washing. He showed them to Von Hebra, who eagerly scanned through the contents.

161

'Ignaz my friend, the whole world must hear about this.'

Semmelweis was cautious, 'I worry about the future, my future here in Vienna. I so very much want to consolidate my work and need the two-year extension of the appointment to be able to do that.'

'I am sure you will be all right.'

'Klein hasn't appeared in the department for weeks but he still has the power to make or break an obstetrician's career.'

Von Hebra's enthusiasm to some extent blinded him to the danger. 'Your work is already valuable and most of your colleagues in the hospital recognize its worth.'

'Thank you for your wonderful support.'

As they were parting Von Hebra said, "That awful dragon, Irma Valerie, was injured in the riots. She's in the surgical ward.'

Semmelweis had good reason to dislike and distrust the woman but his compassion reached out to all who suffered.

'You!' she croaked. She lay on a bed in the surgical ward, which had the appearance of a battlefield. Blood-stained women in dirty clothes crying out in pain and begging for water. Irma Valerie's face was caked in blood and dirt, her respiration rapid and shallow, her left arm clearly broken and placed at a hideous angle across her chest. Broken bone protruded through the skin.

The nurses and doctors were overwhelmed by the sheer scale of the injured, on beds, under beds and between beds on the floor. Ignaz fetched a bowl of warm water, a towel, a comb and laudanum. He put a glass of water to her lips and she drank.

He then set about gently cleaning her face and matted hair, which he also combed. By the time he had applied dressings and pain relief she had a semblance of dignity.

'Thank you, Dr Semmelweis,' she reached out to his face with her right hand, 'I do not deserve your kindness.'

'All the sick and suffering do,' he looked down into her sad eyes, 'I wish you well,' and departed.

Klein also heard that the injured Irma was in the hospital. He sent an administrative official to interview her. 'What did you find out?'

'Nothing. Dr Semmelweis is not involved.' These were the last words she ever spoke.

The April edition of the *Journal of the Medical Society of Vienna* carried a further piece by Dr Ferdinand Von Hebra in which he repeated his earlier description of Semmelweis' discovery. This was followed by quotations from the letters of Professors Michaelis and Tilanus, telling of the sensational results of chlorine hand washing. He appealed to other hospitals to follow the Semmelweis practice and report their data.

A dark cloud began to move across the sun.

39

Vienna – The Curtain Falls

Hektor Arneth had been born in the same year, 1818, as Ignaz Semmelweis and held the equivalent lecturer post in the second obstetric clinic. He was already an active supporter of chlorine hand washing and in mid June 1848 sought out his contemporary in the first clinic.

He found him skilfully completing a difficult breech delivery in which the head of the baby is the last part to emerge and great care is taken to ensure a free airway for the first breath. Semmelweis was being assisted by Charlotte who, by now, was attending to the child. She had become well liked by the frequent visitors to the clinic and formed a popular team with Ignaz. Both were seen as professional, courteous and kind.

'I took over some of the letter-writing burden from Von Hebra and received this strange reply from the professor of obstetrics in Edinburgh, a James Young Simpson.' Hektor handed over the note.

Ignaz dried his hands and read carefully, his brow furrowed. 'He's not very polite, is he?'

'No, and he claims that he knows all about the causes of childbed fever.'

'I think he's a little confused, he does not properly distinguish between contagion and pyaemia. What interests me, Hektor, is the chloroform anaesthetic he first

164

administered last November. We must find out more about it.'

'I'll write back and thank him for his kind observations but concentrate on the anaesthesia.'

'Good idea.' Unknown to Semmelweis, his own countryman Flór Ferenc had used ether in February 1847 at the Saint Rochus Hospital in Pest and was experimenting with chloroform.

The year continued with good results in the obstetric department and Semmelweis made meticulous records. In early September a visiting doctor from the Baltic port and university city of Kiel spoke to the staff of the first obstetric clinic.

He told the sad story of professor Gustav Adolph Michaelis, director of the lying-in hospital. 'Gustav returned from Vienna with such enthusiasm for Dr Semmelweis' discovery and immediately introduced chlorine hand washing with a spectacular reduction in childbed fever.'

Charlotte was listening and remembered Michaelis' mournful expression at the end of Semmelweis' first great teaching round that had changed so much.

'Apparently, shortly before he made the journey to Vienna his cousin, to whom he was very close, died of childbed fever. As time went by he felt more and more responsible and it played so heavily on his mind that on the ninth of August he threw himself under a railway train at the village of Lehrte near Hanover.'

Charlotte repeated the story to Semmelweis and he was deeply touched, since this was one of the men who first had the confidence in his teaching to put it into practice.

Riots continued in the streets in this turbulent year in Vienna. The university had been closed since 26 March and was not re-opened until after 30 October when, in a bloody confrontation, the students and their poor followers were put down.

Semmelweis himself supported the aims of ending imperial autocracy and independence for Hungary. As the time drew near for the extension of his lecturer post Klein emerged from the shadows and disseminated stories of his *bête noire* appearing on ward rounds in revolutionary uniform. In spite of Irma Valerie's last words he did all that was possible to blacken the name of his Hungarian lecturer.

Meanwhile, Ignaz received yet another visitor: Charles Henry Routh was head of the gynaecology department of the Samaritan Free Hospital in London. At the end of their joint ward round on 2 November he said in the presence of doctors, midwives, students and lying-in women, 'Doctor Semmelweis, I congratulate you. What I have seen and heard today is not only a turning point in the care of lying-in women but also the whole field of surgical and gynaecological intervention by the hands of the medical profession. May I continue?'

'Please do,' Hektor Arneth was smiling.

'It is my belief that we are seeing the beginnings of a revolution in worldwide medical thinking and practice. It will long outlive the present political revolutions currently sweeping Europe.'

On 28 November 1848 Routh repeated these views, together with Semmelweis' theory underlying them, in a lecture in London.

There was an overwhelming response throughout Europe and the medical faculty of Vienna proposed to send out a special committee to supervise the practical and scientific implications of Semmelweis' discovery. This was submitted to the Ministry of Public Education on 19 February 1849.

The ministry, in true bureaucratic tradition had convened a committee. In that way no single person could be held responsible for its decision. It was packed with Klein's

166

cronies and as head of the obstetric department it took evidence only from him.

Professor Klein arrived at the ministry at ten o'clock and took his seat at the administrations table. He was not early nor was he late. The well-upholstered chairman knew his role perfectly; a short meeting producing a long report that said nothing but denied the medical faculty its request.

'Well Klein?' No obsequiousness, after all he was only an employee, even though he held the professorial chair in midwifery.

'Thank you, sir. This recommendation by the medical faculty is complete nonsense. It is based on the imaginings of a Hungarian lunatic who has persistently opposed my teachings. He has undermined my proper instruction of students and junior doctors. He has refused to accept the conventional theories of the cause of childbed fever, instead he blames it on doctors carrying material from the autopsy room to the maternity department. Whoever heard of the dead killing the living?' He guffawed at his supposed witticism. 'This proposal is outrageous, particularly as it is based on the mad ideas of a leader of the mob responsible for the recent rioting.'

At last he had struck a chord with the assembled laymen, 'A riot leader, indeed? Chairman, there is no necessity to continue.'

'I agree, no such special supervising body will be authorised.'

Four days later the Medical Society of Vienna invited Semmelweis to discuss his theory of puerperal fever. Klein felt insulted by this honour accorded to Ignaz. Four weeks later Semmelweis' appointment was terminated. Karl Braun took his place.

Ignaz was unemployed and without income but, more important, he did not have access to the work that was not only his lifeblood but also a life-saving activity for the poor women of Vienna and beyond.

On 6 June 1849 he was elected a member of the Medical Society of Vienna sponsored by Rokitanski, Skoda and Von Hebra, but his loss of clinical contact still left him despondent and desolate.

There had also been riots in Hungary and Semmelweis was further depressed to hear that Austrian and Russian troops had occupied Pest on 12 July. There was now a military administration in his country. On receiving this news his spirits took another blow.

For the best part of a year Ignaz applied and reapplied for his old post and was always blocked by Klein. There were high points during this time. In October 1849 Skoda gave a lecture to the Vienna Academy of Sciences, which gained support for Semmelweis but also released jealousy. During his overview of puerperal fever he had mentioned the high incidence in Prague and earned the enmity of Wilhelm Scanzoni, who subsequently published a number of papers attacking chlorine hand washing.

After further failed applications, which were now blocked by the Ministry of Public Education, Ignaz gave a lecture on the origin of puerperal fever with Rokitanski in the chair. The lecture was well attended, including Arneth, Skoda and Von Hebra in the audience. He concluded, 'And so, gentlemen, childbed fever is spread by doctors' hands and instruments contaminated by decaying organic matter which enters the bloodstream of lying-in women via the damaged genital tract. There follows pyaemia and death.'

'*Quod erat demonstrandum*,' Rokitanski was final. Muted opposition came from Eduard Lumpe, Semmelweis' predecessor, who said that since it was seasonal there had to be, as taught by Klein, an atmospheric cause. The room remained silent.

The lecture took place in May 1850 and in October Ignaz was offered a junior post in theoretical obstetrics. No access to lying-in women, no midwifery duties, no contact with practical problems – all he had was poorly constructed mannequins.

This was, for Ignaz, the time to seek outside help. He knocked on the door of number ten Maria Theresien Strasse and to his surprise it was opened by Charlotte, with five-year-old Alexandra holding on to her other hand.

'Dr Semmelweis.'

'Miss Weiss.'

They were equally surprised. 'Please come in.'

'Is Mr Rudolf Orlov at home?'

'He is indeed.'

Edith appeared from the front room. 'Welcome, let me take your coat.' She ushered him through the door and he shook hands with Rudolf Orlov. Charlotte, Edith and an excited Alexandra joined them and everyone sat down.

'Dr Semmelweis, I am pleased but not surprised to see you. I would have liked to talk to you before now, but I felt you had to come in your own time.'

'You know what has been going on?' Ignaz was gaunt, he had lost weight and was neither eating nor sleeping properly.

'Charlotte has reported everything. You are in an impossible position. You have made a great discovery for which you are hated by the old guard and profoundly admired by the up and coming members of your profession.'

'You make it sound so simple.' Ignaz listened to Rudolf intently.

'It is. You should leave Vienna.'

'Why?'

'Every day you stay here diminishes your achievement, reduces your will to go on and damages your physical and mental health.'

'You put it very strongly.'

169

'Do not delay, I fear for your future.'

Charlotte felt she had to speak. 'Please listen to Rudolf, Dr Semmelweis, he knows what is happening here in Vienna. We have discussed every option.'

Edith also felt moved to say something. 'Dr Semmelweis, through Charlotte and our own observations we know you are a great man. Please, please do not stay to be destroyed in Vienna.' Semmelweis stood up; Edith embraced him and whispered, 'I beg of you, leave Vienna.'

On 27 October 1850 Dr Ignaz Semmelweis boarded the railway train for Pest. He had told no one of his departure. He left behind him a professor who would always be remembered for having attempted to engineer the destruction of the brightest star in the obstetric sky.

Two days later, Charlotte was again sitting in the front room of number ten with Rudolf.

'You will go too?'

'Yes.'

'I thought so, he needs your help and very professional support. Can you leave Alexandra?'

'I'll be all right with Edith,' the little voice came from behind Charlotte's chair.

40

Saint Rochus Hospital

A solitary figure stood on the platform of the new railway station at Györ in north-west Hungary. Lajos Markusovszky had decided to meet his friend half way along his journey to Pest and Buda. He had felt humiliated by the threatening presence of the Austrian and Russian military. Curt demands for identification together with rough handling of civilians by soldiers, which has characterised armed occupations throughout history.

The railway train pulled to a halt, exactly on time at five minutes past midday in driving rain. Lajos boarded one of the carriages and quickly found his close friend and colleague. Ignaz was amazed and delighted to see this very familiar face. They embraced.

'God, you look awful,' Lajos smiled.

'I feel as I look,' was the gloomy reply.

'I got your telegram.'

'I'm glad I sent it, thank you for meeting me.' The train moved towards Buda and Pest.

During the remaining journey Ignaz told his closest friend all that had taken place in Vienna since they had last been together; concluding with his visit to Rudolf Orlov and the advice he had received.

'He was both perceptive and right.'

'He has a civilian job with the imperial army. Even they

171

know about Klein and the obstetric department.'

'You've made a wise move, Ignaz, and it's a great scientific loss for Vienna. Although things haven't been good here in Hungary you'll be able to continue your proper research.'

'How are things in the obstetric department?'

'Not as I or you would like. Professor Ede Flórián Birly has been in charge for over thirty years. He is a good man, particularly as a practical obstetrician, exercising patience rather than rushing to interfere. Standards have risen, but midwifery is still not compulsory for medical students.'

'What are his views about childbed fever?'

'He believes it is an intestinal disturbance. You will find out more tomorrow evening.'

'What have you arranged?'

'We have been invited to the home of my chief, Professor János Balassa. He is an amazing head of the surgical unit. He was politically active at the time of the riots and put in gaol. This provoked enormous student protest and the authorities were forced to release him after three months but one of these ludicrous government commissions removed him from his professorial chair and it was only restored to him by a royal amnesty.'

'Disease is not our only problem; bureaucratic interference is everywhere.' Ignaz spoke for his profession in 1850. He would have been horrified to look into the future.

They arrived in Pest and set off to find some temporary accommodation. Semmelweis admitted to himself that his departure from Vienna, where he had done so much and felt his work far from finished, marked a low point. He was depressed, but neither deranged nor defeated.

The following evening Markusovszky introduced him to János Balassa. He was impressed with the tall, dark-haired, eloquent professor who greeted him with a firm handshake and a smile.

172

'Welcome to our little circle, Dr Semmelweis. You may find things somewhat suppressed here in Hungary. We lost our bid for independence and medicine suffers in the same way as everything else.'

'It is a pleasure to meet you,' Ignaz guessed that his host was only about four years older than himself.

'My nephew, Flór, told me all about the archives and the contretemps that occurred beforehand. He is still very embarrassed, but you have a lifelong admirer there.'

'He really is a very nice young man, Professor.'

Ignaz had memories of the dusty student carrying huge piles of old papers, some of which were covered in green mould. 'His wild energies were put to good use.'

'I'm glad to hear it,' Janos laughed. 'come and meet Ignaz Hirschler, he will tell you more of our situation here.' Semmelweis recognised the face and remembered that this had been the unfortunate doctor who had pointlessly been brought in to make up the numbers when he had been appointed lecturer over four years previously. 'He is making great strides in classifying eye diseases.'

The two Ignazes shook hands. 'I feel very embarrassed that you had your time wasted at that interview.'

'Think nothing of it. I was irritated and baffled at the time but I put it down to experience. Anyway, my only suit needed cleaning. I have read of your work in the Vienna Medical Journal and felt you should meet Professor Ede Flórian Birly at the Pest medical faculty obstetric clinic the day after tomorrow. There are some medical students there, but only on a voluntary basis.'

'That is very kind of you.'

'Most of the maternity cases go there but in the summer holiday months they are admitted to the Saint Rochus Hospital, and it has been having a terrible outbreak of childbed fever.'

'I shall go there tomorrow.' Ignaz Semmelweis was

animated at the prospect of being back in his area of expertise, particularly if he could help with the problem of childbed fever.

The Saint Rochus Hospital and adjoining church had been opened amidst celebrations on 29 May 1798. It was to be found in a square off Korepesi Street, which was to become Rákoczi Street, not far from the east bank of the Danube. It was expanded in 1838 to a large modern hospital of 600 beds.

The saint, according to legend, suffered from the plague and is depicted in a pilgrim's robe, which he lifts and points to an ulcer on his right thigh. He worked miracles among fellow sufferers and was accompanied by a dog bringing bread; an angel touched and cured the sore.

The following day Ignaz visited the hospital and was surprised to find the surgical and lying-in women in together. There were no medical students and the doctors performed post-mortems. Childbed fever was rife. Ward rounds started with surgical cases, leaving the obstetric cases until last.

A few days later he was courteously received by Professor Birly at the obstetric clinic of the Pest medical faculty, where medical students were given instruction on a voluntary basis.

'You are welcome, Dr Semmelweis. I am familiar with your work but have always felt that childbed fever is due to an intestinal affliction, which is greatly helped by purges.'

Semmelweis was not going to upset this respected obstetrician. 'I quite understand, sir, but I would be most grateful to work in your department.'

'Dr Semmelweis, you come to us here in Hungary at a very difficult time. I am sixty-three years old and have been professor here at the Pest medical faculty for over thirty years. Our bid for political independence has ended in defeat. With military domination has come cultural

174

and scientific suppression. The medical society of Pest–Buda has been closed and leading medical men imprisoned. We have been deprived of money and outside contact with the advancing medical world. I have never before witnessed such silence and stagnation.'

Ignaz listened carefully to this terrible story, 'You paint a black picture, Professor. How may I be of help?'

'I would like you to take over the maternity department of the Saint Rochus Hospital. We very much need your experience, knowledge and renowned energy. However, such an appointment will have to be in an honorary capacity, without pay.' Birly spread his hands and grimaced in a hopeless and apologetic gesture.

On 17 November 1850 Semmelweis submitted his application, in Hungarian, to Ferenc Koller, regional sheriff of Pest–Buda. The letter, including his *curriculum vitae*, was formal but not obsequious. It contained two notable phrases: 'My obstetrical work in Vienna did not remain unknown to the medical world' and 'I will do my best to keep down the necessary expenses.'

The *Vienna Medical Weekly Journal* carried a notice in its first issue of 1851. 'The well known Dr Semmelweis has been appointed lecturer at the Saint Rochus Hospital in the University of Pest under Professor Birly.'

Opposition to Semmelweis' appointment by the director of the Saint Rochus Hospital became known to Von Hebra. 'I will put an end to all these injustices,' he told Skoda. 'We know his worth and have tried to support him here in Vienna, he must not be thwarted in Pest–Buda.'

'We still have the power of print, the Austrian authorities have closed down all Hungarian publications.'

Semmelweis received official notification of his unsalaried assignment on 12 March and commenced his duties on 20 May 1851.

Meanwhile Charlotte received a letter from Erzsébet

Ruprecht, the head of midwifery in Pest, confirming her appointment as senior midwife at the Saint Rochus Hospital.

41

Small Acorns

Charlotte arrived in Pest on 20 June 1851, the day after Alexandra's sixth birthday. There had been laughter and tears but above all agreement for the move to Hungary in support of Dr Semmelweis.

The country in which she now found herself, was in theory still governed by Emperor Franzis Joseph from Vienna, military rule supported by Russia. The language of the university and hospitals was German, as in Vienna, but these institutions were suffering financially and politically – all armies cost a lot of money, other people's money.

A one-horse carriage was being attended by a watering girl wearing a yellow headscarf; when the horse's thirst was quenched they set off towards the fifty-three-year-old almshouse that had been expanded and developed into the Saint Rochus Hospital administered by and on behalf of the people of the city of Pest.

Erzsébet Ruprecht and Ignaz Semmelweis met her just inside the great black wooden doors.

'Welcome, Miss Weiss.' Erzsébet's greeting was warm and sincere.

Semmelweis gave a formal bow, 'It is a pleasure to have you on the staff.'

'Miss Weiss, I will show you to your room but I am sure you appreciate this is not Vienna.'

'I know, the devastation and poverty that come with war were only too evident on the streets as I came to the hospital. It is, of course, the human cost that is the greatest. Amputated limbs mean no work, dead fathers mean no money and fat generals mean social injustice.'

'You're very perceptive, Miss Weiss.'

'I do not expect luxury, but would like to unpack. I have brought my own uniform.'

Ignaz had listened respectfully, 'When you are ready I will give you the tour.' He smiled encouragingly and left the two women and gave his usual formal slight bow.

'Come,' Erzsébet led the way to a staircase.

'How do I address you?'

'Matron will be fine.' They climbed the four flights of stairs to a corridor in the attic. She opened a door into a small bare room containing only a bed, chair and tiny window. 'I apologise for such poor accommodation.'

'It's fine, I've been in worse, much worse.' The thought of that dreadful Vienna doss house flashed through her mind, 'I will soon make it cosy.'

'We have a dining room but as I told you in my letter there may be—' she smiled bleakly, 'will be delays with money.'

Charlotte felt she had in turn to reassure this woman for whom she had an increasing respect, 'Matron that is not my reason for being here.'

'Thank you for your understanding. I think you will be tired after your journey, I will leave you now and arrange your tour of the hospital tomorrow morning.' She hesitated at the door, 'I have to ask you a question,' she was embarrassed.

'It's all right, I have been asked it before.'

'Suzanne Lafkrantz gave you a glowing reference; she said you were the best midwife it had ever been her privilege to teach.'

178

'I can repay her a little now,' Charlotte simply said. 'Dr Semmelweis gave me two things: my life and my dignity, neither of which I intend to sacrifice.'

'Then I don't need to ask the question.'

'Exactly and thank you,' she paused a moment. 'But there is something about him I would like to say.'

'I will, of course, respect anything said in confidence.'

'I have seen Dr Semmelweis work in the maternity department in Vienna for five years. He was deeply moved by the suffering and death from childbed fever. He seemed to be tireless in his clinical work, his research and reviewing all the possible causes of what is usually a fatal condition. In simple terms, that I understand, he concluded that the disease was due to the transfer of decaying organic matter to the already bruised and sometimes lacerated vagina and uterus of lying-in women. Most usually this transfer is made by the hands of doctors who perform autopsies before attending the mothers.'

'Not a popular thesis.'

'Definitely not, but by introducing chlorine hand washing there has been a dramatic fall in the incidence of childbed fever in the first obstetric clinic in the Vienna General Hospital.'

'And so he lost his job?'

'Yes.'

'We need careful diplomacy. Professor Birly is much respected and has a good record in this area.'

'I shall watch my step.' Charlotte felt she had an ally.

On the bright sunny morning of 21 June she found Dr Ignaz Semmelweis waiting for her at eight o'clock in the main entrance of the Saint Rochus Hospital.

'You are an early riser, doctor.'

'I like to think of myself as a postman – I bring prompt and trouble-free deliveries. Shall I lead the way?'

'Please do.'

He bounded up the stairs to the combined surgical, gynaecological and maternity section. Charlotte noticed the renewed energy and enthusiasm; she was a little breathless when they entered the ward for seventy-five women. Near the door, where ward rounds commenced, they passed a variety of problems: broken bones that had been set, drained abscesses and a few abdominal operations. Wounds were being dressed and pain relieved. The beds were old, close together and the smell, that smell Charlotte had almost forgotten, was pervasive.

As they passed the women who were recovering from abdominal operations Semmelweis remarked, 'What you see may not be perfect but we have one wonderful advantage here at Saint Rochus.' They stopped at the end of the bed of a young woman with an open wound in the right lower quadrant of her abdomen being dressed. 'A gangrenous perforated appendix was removed and drained two days ago by Dr Markusovszky. This was only possible because she was given a general anaesthetic by Dr Flór Ferenc. He first used ether on 12 February 1847 but now chloroform anaesthesia is regularly in use in this hospital.'

Charlotte was impressed, 'Without surgery – ?'

'She would have died.' He was pleased to show her something positive. 'Let us move on to our section.' In the far end of the room was a further mixture of conditions, miscarriages both natural and criminal, the venereal diseases gonorrhoea and syphilis, complicated birth injuries slowly healing and lying-in women. There was a smell here, it was the welcome one of chlorine.

'You have started the hand washing.'

'Yes, and next week we move all our gynaecological and obstetric women into a separate ward. Professor Birly has supported me in finding separate accommodation. It wasn't easy.'

'Change never is.'

'Miss Weiss, you may find our situation in the Pest medical community very different from Vienna. I certainly do.' Just a hint of irritability showed through his previous enthusiasm.

She laid a hand on his right forearm, 'Dr Semmelweis, although I am a midwife by training I am also a nurse and a human being. You know you have my support whatever the circumstances.'

'In our new ward we will be admitting obstetric cases during July and August, holidays and between university term times. For the remainder of the year lying-in women are to be admitted to the university clinic under Professor Birly. Unfortunately the numbers will be small but we will show the benefits of chlorine hand washing. The city fathers do not yet see teaching and curing as compatible functions.'

Charlotte cheerily replied, 'Little acorns grow into fine big oak trees.'

Semmelweis' spirits rose, 'Yes.'

42

Professor

Under the supervision of its honorary head physician, Dr Ignaz Semmelweis, routine chlorine hand washing was introduced into the new obstetric section of the Saint Rochus Hospital. There was an immediate and dramatic fall in the occurrence of childbed fever.

During the years 1851–1857 there were 933 deliveries and only eight deaths from puerperal fever, less than one per cent.

János Balassa and Lajos Markusovszky frequently asked Ignaz to publish these results. They were just as frequently met with the reply, 'I am confident that the truth of this matter will soon be recognised.'

In Vienna Karl Braun never mentioned Semmelweis' name either to students or in his book of 1854 *The Puerperal Process*. Ignaz found this hurtful but not devastating. In fact these were happy and rewarding years. The Balassa circle met regularly and provided tremendous intellectual stimulation. In spite of the suppression of Hungarian publications the library was well supplied with medical journals.

A paper by Professor Eduard Siebold in 1852 proposing that venereal disease played a part in childbed fever prompted Semmelweis to invite the obstetrician from Göttingen to visit Pest. He did and subsequently wrote a detailed account of his visit and the part chlorine hand washing played in the prophylaxis of puerperal fever.

Ignaz remained unsalaried and like any normal human being he had to earn a living. Private obstetric practice was his only option now that his inheritance had been used up.

He prospered, as he was sure to do with his natural gentle, kind and thoughtful approach but his great achievement in eliminating the reality and fear of childbed fever sealed his success.

Professor Ede Flórian Birly died on 25 November 1854. The impact on Ignaz' private practice was immediate. Birly had been hugely respected and his patients quickly sought out Dr Semmelweis.

This was welcome but Ignaz was wary of the future. As in the past he confided in Markusovszky, 'Lajos, Vienna is the problem, this is a Ministry of Public Education appointment by the central government. They are bound to dig up something to throw at me. I didn't leave the city in a blaze of glory.'

'You still have great supporters and admirers of your work in Vienna. The influence of Von Hebra, Skoda and Rokitanski is rising and the imperial government disintegrates before our eyes.'

'I don't think I could go through all the applying, re-applying and time wasting uncertainty again.'

'You won't have to.'

'How can you know that?'

Markusovszky did not reply but he did smile.

The Ministry of Public Education announced in December 1854 that the vacancy for the late Professor Birly's chair in obstetrics in Pest would be filled on 20 February 1855. There were seven short-listed candidates including Karl Braun and Ignaz Semmelweis. The announcement appeared in the *Vienna Medical Weekly*.

Amazingly, an anonymous letter from Pest appeared in the same journal on 1 February 1855. That was three weeks before the Pest medical faculty was to meet to discuss the candidature. The letter read:

'Pest University has agreed to the appointment of Dr Ignaz Semmelweis to the chair of midwifery. His theoretical and practical training will open a new epoch in midwifery in Hungary.'

There was much huffing and puffing and the medical faculty of the University of Pest finally convened on 20 March 1855. The Pest Letter, as it became known, caused consternation and instead of a proper discussion a ballot was proposed. Karl Braun came first and Semmelweis second.

'This is outrageous,' Professor Zsigmond Schordann, a physiologist well known for his opposition to the selection of medical students on the basis of family connections, was fuming. 'Braun has deliberately slighted Dr Semmelweis and persuaded Scanzoni in Würtzburg to speak out against chlorine hand washing.' He looked around him at the eyes staring at the table, 'Braun does not even speak Hungarian and he is not likely to in six weeks' time.' No one spoke, Schordann persisted, 'We have here in Pest an outstanding Hungarian candidate. Dr Semmelweis has a European reputation after pioneering work in the field of childbed fever both in Vienna and here in Pest.'

In true committee tradition the matter was passed to the university council for a decision, they in turn passed it to the presidential council, which sought the advice of the chief of police, the civil and military governors of Hungary and it finally landed back in the Ministry of Public Education in Vienna. This farce could not go on for ever. On 18 July 1855 the King appointed Ignaz Semmelweis professor of theoretical and practical obstetrics in the University of Pest.

He took the appointment oath on 27 August and commenced his duties on the thirtieth. He now had a large number of patients under his care and he gave them enthusiastic, determined and devoted attention.

There were problems: money, the continued domination of Vienna, the small dark rooms for between six and twelve beds in the institute for obstetrics on the second floor; there was no lecture room for students and nurses, teaching took place in corridors and ventilation was bad and close to the garbage facility; women could only be admitted once labour had commenced.

Semmelweis made petitions, coaxed, cajoled and sought public support at functions such as formal balls and dinners.

He succeeded and in 1857 out of 514 deliveries at the institute and Saint Rochus Hospital there were only two deaths from childbed fever.

He was honoured by being asked to deliver the child of Elizabeth, daughter of feudal Lord Joseph of Brno. He was chosen over rivals from Vienna and Pest.

On 14 January 1857 he accompanied Lajos Markusovszky to a ball in the Royal Palace on castle hill in Buda. Mária Weidenhoffer also attended with her father Ignaz.

43

Blue and White Dress

It was a glittering occasion in the ballroom of the 500-year-old building overlooking Buda, the west bank of the Danube and coincidentally Semmelweis' birthplace in Apród Street. This great building had suffered repeated occupations but the resilient Hungarians were expert at restoration.

This event was sponsored by the Mayor of Buda and his council, which consisted of merchants, shipbuilders and bankers. Its purpose was to raise money for the welfare of the destitute, homeless and disabled; the real casualties of any war.

Ignaz and Lajos were enthusiastic supporters of these social gatherings. They were smartly turned out in black frock coats, white bow ties and waistcoats.

'Lajos, who is that striking young woman with long black hair in the blue dress?'

'I don't know, but I do know the man with her. His name is Ignaz Weidenhoffer, he is a merchant on the city council. A few months ago he had a very large painful perianal abscess which I treated. He was extremely grateful.'

'I am not surprised.'

'Would you like to meet them?

They walked over to the middle-aged man and his elegant companion. She was wearing a sky-blue dress,

186

which had a full skirt, short sleeves and a white horizontal lace decoration. Her shoulders were bare and the second row of the trimming dipped down into a vee at the narrow waist. 'Good evening, Mr Weidenhoffer. I trust you are in good health?'

'Good evening, Dr Markusovszky. I have now fully recovered, thank you.'

'May I present my friend and colleague Professor Ignaz Semmelweis.' The two men gave slight formal bows.

'It is indeed a pleasure, Professor. May I now present my daughter, Maria.'

'Good evening, gentlemen,' Maria gave a little curtsy. 'My friend Giselle Von Hebra is the daughter of your great supporter in Vienna, Professor Semmelweis.'

'He certainly is a wonderful colleague. How did you meet his daughter?'

'We were at school together. When I was ten I went to stay with her in Vienna. We were taken to see Jenny Lind in *The Daughter of the Regiment*, she was amazing. Dr Von Hebra said that you are amazing as well,' the smile was charming and a little mischievous.

Ignaz blushed but was pleased with the compliment, 'I would be honoured, Maria, if you would dance with me.'

'I would be delighted.'

They moved away. 'You have a beautiful daughter, Mr Weidenhoffer.' Markusovszky was a little envious.

'She gets that from her mother. Maria also has a lovely loyal nature. The man she marries will have to be a dedicated partner, her delicate features belie a strong will.'

The orchestra launched into one of the many waltzes of Johann Strauss, which were just as popular in Buda and Pest as they were in Vienna. Semmelweis was apprehensive that he was too poorly skilled on the ballroom floor to please this enchanting woman, he held her lightly, 'You must excuse my lack of expertise, Miss Weidenhoffer.'

187

Maria laughed, 'You have a light step, Professor, my toes feel quite safe.'

'Ignaz, please. I may be thirty-nine years old but I would be honoured if you would treat me as an equal.'

Her laugh was infectious and gently chiding, 'I am Maria, no more Miss Weidenhoffer, and I like being your friend.'

The ice was broken and against custom they remained in each other's company for the remainder of the evening.

The affection between Maria and Ignaz grew and he received a warm welcome into the Weidenhoffer family circle. She listened to his story, his difficulties, his ideas, his hopes and of course his passionate concern for the sufferers of childbed fever. Her listening was her gift to him, which he gladly accepted. With the happy approval of friends and relatives the marriage of Maria Weidenhoffer and Ignaz Semmelweis was arranged for 1 June 1857.

During the period of their engagement news from Vienna reported the death of Professor Johann Klein. Semmelweis sent a letter of condolence to his late antagonist's family; he made no mention of their professional disagreements.

Six specialists in Vienna wrote to Semmelweis entreating him to apply for Klein's job. 'Ignaz, you are happy and successful here, Vienna is poison for you.' Markusovszky was right; he was not even short-listed for the appointment. There was a collective sigh of relief in Pest–Buda. In their fragile wisdom the authorities appointed Karl Braun to succeed the man who tried and failed to destroy Ignaz Semmelweis.

It was no coincidence that at Braun's instigation József Fletscher wrote a letter to the *Obstetric Journal of Vienna* stating, 'It is time to stop all this nonsense of chlorine hand washing.' Semmelweis was hurt but said nothing. Markusovszky was outraged, 'That toxic troublemaker Braun is doing this purely out of a sense of petty revenge for not getting the Pest professorial chair.' They sat together in a Pest café near the Saint Rochus Hospital. 'Klein belonged to an old world of non-scientific theory but Braun is attacking you personally out of sheer spite. He cares nothing for the women who will suffer, only for his vanity.'

'You're right, but I am sure the truth of childbed fever and its prevention will become widely accepted,' he smiled, 'and I am getting married next week.'

Markusovszky smiled, 'So you are.'

The marriage of Maria Weidenhoffer and Ignaz Semmelweis took place at eleven o'clock on the morning of 1 June 1857 at the Krieztinaváros church in Buda.

Among the guests who were warmly welcomed by the couple were Charlotte Weiss and her twelve-year-old daughter Alexandra, Rudolf Orlov, his two daughters, Georgina, twenty-two, Kate, sixteen and his son Franz, nineteen, and lastly but not least, Edith. Semmelweis kissed Edith on each cheek and introduced her to Maria.

'It is a wonderful day, Professor Semmelweis,' Edith smiled, 'for everyone.'

44

Resilience in Adversity

Professor Ignaz Semmelweis enjoyed both love and respect in Hungary. Maria only asked once, 'Do you ever feel you would like to return to Vienna?'

'Never. Rudolf Orlov did me a great service when he advised me to return to Pest,' he grinned, 'neither of us knew that you would be here for me.'

'I always will be here for you. Please tell me everything that happens in your work, both good and bad.' She took a deep breath, desperately searching for the right words to ensure that nothing should intrude on their happiness. 'You are my husband and nothing can be so bad that it has to stay sealed inside your beautiful mind.'

'Nothing ever will.'

'We may be a little restricted in these cramped rooms, but it's home, and it makes me easy to find,' her eyes twinkled as she surveyed their small apartment in Hatvani Street, which later became Kossuth Lajos Street.

When Semmelweis was appointed to the professorial chair in obstetrics in 1855 he retained his honorary appointment at Saint Rochus Hospital. He was deeply devoted to his work there, which had restored his dignity and health. He had raised the reputation of the maternity department and largely eradicated childbed fever. No one had questioned his ability to continue his honorary duties together with directing the institute of obstetrics.

In late August 1857 a letter was delivered to his home from the Ministry of Culture in Vienna. Ignaz opened it, 'Extraordinary!'

'What is it?' Maria saw his mixture of puzzlement and anger.

'A complaint by a Dr Rott.'

'Who is he?'

'A Pest general practitioner. He wrote to the presidential council and maintained that I cannot be both a state and a municipal employee.'

'That's splitting hairs,' Maria was indignant on her husband's behalf, 'Rott by name and rotten by nature. What will you do?'

'I have to resign from Saint Rochus.'

'You've made a wonderful change there and the hospital will always be grateful, you will never be forgotten.'

The news of the departure of Semmelweis was received with indignation in the Saint Rochus Hospital; Charlotte, who was now the senior midwife in the maternity unit, was unusually vehement, 'What incredible pettiness, envy and jealousy have stalked Dr Semmelweis from Vienna to Pest.'

In the first two years of marriage Ignaz and Maria had two children, given the names of their mother and father, who sadly died in infancy. The couple grieved privately and looked forward to the children they knew they would have in the future.

'Let us use this time and your energy to improve the institute of obstetrics. You have the poor facilities of small dark rooms, nowhere for teaching and you believe that recent erysipelas outbreak was in part due to these conditions.'

'What should I do?' Semmelweis was increasingly respectful of Maria's judgement.

191

'Request an audience with the Governor of Hungary.'

'Prince Albrecht?'

'That's the one.'

He followed her advice and was amazed at the speed of change. Within a few weeks the institute of obstetrics and gynaecology had moved from its dark confined quarters in Új Világ Street to the well-lit, spacious Kunewalder warehouse in Országút.

He was also learning, with the forceful advice of Maria, how to deal with administrators. There was a desperate need for new bedsheets. He had the dirty disintegrating linen delivered to the office of Joseph Tadler, a presidential councillor. This little donation was repeated regularly: at one stage poor Joseph could not see out of his office window. Eventually 300 new sheets miraculously arrived at the institute.

The laundering of bed linen was a constant source of problems. Carelessness made shortages worse. On one occasion in 1857, shortly before leaving Saint Rochus Hospital there was a sudden rise in the incidence of childbed fever. Charlotte spoke to Semmelweis.

'I have to tell you, doctor, that I have seen Nurse Narina Nemeth repeatedly putting the soiled sheets from the beds of one of the very few women who have died from childbed fever on to a bed prepared for a new patient in labour.'

'Thank you for telling me,' Semmelweis was intolerant of equals who should know better, but did not victimise junior staff. 'It may well be that she thinks we no longer have a problem. Please explain that where we have contamination we still need vigilance.' He showed kindness to honest mistakes.

The problem was solved, for the time being.

His position forced him to be responsible for medical expenditure. He did not welcome this extra burden. He did not forgive disloyalty particularly from high officials.

192

'You, Dr Semmelweis, are overspending on linen and staff and she,' the officious Joseph Tadler pointed at Erzsébet Ruprecht, 'is in a conspiracy with you.'

Ignaz was outraged. Erzsébet laid a hand on his threatening arm, 'Be calm, doctor, this is a matter for the presidential council.' Tadler was very unhappy and his superiors were informed that his intervention was likely to cause a return to the large numbers of deaths from childbed fever. No such interference came from that particular individual.

Semmelweis and his young progressive colleagues within the János Balassa circle were opposed by the old guard of the medical faculty. The new group were in favour of a central medical building. They were supported by an editorial in the *Vienna Medical Weekly*.

The editor wrote,

Professors János Balassa, Ignaz Semmelweis and their forward looking colleagues are to visit Vienna in April 1859 to address the Ministry of Public Education. They will be petitioning for a central medical building to unite the teaching, research and provision of care within the University of Pest, we support this concept. However we note the opposition led by Professor Lajos Tognio, head of the incongruously linked departments of pharmacology and pathology. We fear that his desire to maintain the isolation of his little empire will successfully stand in the way of progress.

On their train journey back from Vienna Semmelweis was philosophical, 'János, I am not depressed with our failure today. I believe that in spite of Tognio and his fellow dinosaurs time will be on our side.' He reflected on his own situation. 'In the same way I have faith

193

that the truth about the concept, aetiology and prophylaxis of childbed fever will soon be known and widely
accepted.'

45

Happiness and Enthusiastic Activity

In the medical faculty of Pest, Semmelweis was seen as lively, young and energetic. Qualities admired by Charlotte as well as her midwife colleagues, valued by Professor János Balassa, head of surgery and chairman of the university committee, and seen as a passport to a safe delivery by his lying-in women.

Autumn 1858 had seen Ignaz being offered the prestigious professorial chair in Obstetrics in Zurich. As he considered the proposition in their new more spacious apartment near the institute, Maria answered a knock on the front door. Lajos Markusovszky always seemed to arrive at the right moment.

'Do come in, Marko, Ignaz truly needs your opinion.'

Semmelweis showed Markusovszky the letter from the Zurich medical faculty. 'It is a tempting thought, Ignaz, a luxury department, superb research facilities, access to the top academic platforms in Europe. Your work and teaching would be widely and accurately publicised, it seems perfect.'

'Do you really mean that, Lajos?' She looked at him in amazement.

'No, I am playing the devil's advocate. I very definitely mean "no".' His smile was reassuring.

'How do you truly see things?' Once again it was Maria who spoke.

'Ignaz, you have made the teaching of obstetrics to medical students compulsory, you have established an improved medical library, a restoration of medical publishing, a thriving professional department in a new atmosphere of scientific progress, but above all you have had an earth-shattering impact on childbed fever.'

'I thank you my friend, I know you're right.'

Maria was both delighted and relieved but she knew this was the moment to voice a worry she had held for some time. 'Ignaz, if you leave Hungary your enemies will see it as a sign of weakness.'

Markusovszky was quick to follow her lead, 'Braun in Vienna has not promoted the proper use of chlorine hand washing and childbed fever still ravages lying-in women there. He and Scanzoni will see a move by you as weakness.'

'I agree. I should stay here in my home country where I have the supreme luxury of my teaching being appreciated and practised. Not everyone in history has had that privilege,' Semmelweis was relieved to have the support of Markusovszky and Maria in this difficult decision. He smiled, 'Is there anything else to say, Lajos?'

'You know there is, Ignaz.'

'This time, I am listening.'

Lajos leaned forward in his chair, 'The time for editorials, letters and short papers in journals is over. Your chlorine hand washing, with the theory and research behind it, has to be published as a book.'

Maria listened in silent approval.

Semmelweis' shoulders dropped slightly. 'It will take a long time, there is so much detail, so many cases and deaths to review. The post-mortem work will be crucial as well as the elimination of all the old theories.'

It was a daunting task. Semmelweis frequently discussed progress and his thoughts on how he could get the work done. 'I believe that I have to give my brain a rest from childbed fever from time to time. I must do other things, including my duties in the institute to keep my focus on all that has happened to crystallize my ideas.'

His practical work and teaching in the institute continued as before but he spent increasing amounts of time in the library, which had been, in part, his creation.

His output was phenomenal; among his many lectures to the Medical Society in Pest were such varied subjects as 'Spontaneous amputation of limbs of foetuses due to amniotic fasciculi or adhesions', and 'Caesarian birth in women with rickets'. He also discussed in graphic detail, 'Labour in the presence of a massive ovarian cyst.'

He published accounts of operations in the newly resurrected *Hungarian Weekly Medical Journal*. This was a great achievement in the face of continued oppression. These operations were sometimes performed with János Balassa and facilitated by the anaesthetic of Dr Flór Ferenc. They included, 'Myomectomy: the removal of a fibroid in the seventh month of pregnancy' and 'Operations for ovarian tumours'.

Semmelweis started his book in March 1859, and the completed work was presented to the Hungarian Academy of Sciences on 27 November 1860.

During this time his preparatory studies led him to issue clear instructions on chlorine hand washing. He used the opportunity to do this on his Grand Round at the end of April 1859. He paused after examining a lying-in woman whose cervix had been crushed by a difficult forceps delivery and before proceeding to a lady who had a straightforward delivery.

'Ladies and gentlemen—' this weekly event now regularly attracted a huge attendance. Those present included Charlotte, who brought her midwives and students from the Saint Rochus Hospital. 'Here we have a clear example of why there must be chlorine hand washing between each of the lying-in women.' Not a foot shuffled, not a paper rustled and not a cough was emitted; the gathering was as silent and attentive as an opera audience during a dramatic aria.

'The lady I have just examined has devitalised tissue that may have released decaying organic material on to my hands. The next lady has healthy tissues, although they are almost certainly bruised with tiny tears in the living membranes. This lying-in woman is well but vulnerable.'

Semmelweis then performed a chlorine hand wash before approaching the woman, 'I must not introduce decaying organic matter into the bloodstream of this lady via her healing tissues.' Some of the onlooker's eyebrows were raised in surprise but the silence was maintained.

'Although the majority of women with childbed fever have initially been contaminated by doctors' hands having come straight from the post-mortem, it is possible to transfer the causative agent from one living woman to another. The rule will now be chlorine hand washing before examining all patients and, of course, before leaving the ward.' There were no questions, no quibbles and no niggling objections; the logic and the solution were abundantly clear.

His book was written in German to reach the widest possible audience. Semmelweis clarified his thoughts by delivering four lectures on the cause of puerperal fever to the Medical Society of Pest–Buda in the summer months of 1859.

46

Reaction

Ignaz' book was ready for press on 30 August 1860 and published in October. It was presented to the Hungarian Academy of Sciences on 27 November and reviewed by Lajos Markusovszky in the *Vienna Medical Weekly*. He praised the work: 'Dr Semmelweis' publication has been based on clinical observations, statistics and research. The only logical conclusion must be, that puerperal fever is caused by decaying organic matter transmitted through the injured genitals into the bloodstream of lying-in women. It is destroyed by chlorine hand washing.'

He scathingly attacked 'Old theories, dreamed up in ivory towers [that] lead to bias and petty jealousies.'

Reactions throughout the world were predictably polarised. Ignaz seasoned supporters and admirers reported wonderful reductions in puerperal fever as a result of chlorine hand washing. They were joined by others, including J.A.J. Pippinsköld from far away Helsinki.

Nevertheless the old antagonists in Vienna and Würzburg were unmoved. As the months passed by it seemed that there was united opposition to him both personally and to his teachings.

Margit, his first child to survive, was born on 8 May 1861. He and Maria were thrilled. Within a few days they were visited by Charlotte and Lajos Markusovszky.

'You have a beautiful daughter, Dr Semmelweis, I am so very pleased for you and Maria.' Charlotte held the baby, 'You have achieved a new safety and future for all mothers and babies – I think Margit is a fitting reward.'

Markusovszky tickled the little girl under the chin, 'Hello, young lady, you have a famous father!'

'If only that was so, Lajos. I breathed a huge sigh of relief when I finished the book; I thought the proof and remedy were there in print and when people saw it plainly before their eyes there could be no further objections. On the contrary it seems to have made things worse in some quarters.'

'Dr Semmelweis, I and the other midwives here in Pest have read your book. We have seen how chlorine hand washing means that we no longer have the hopeless task of nursing dying mothers with childbed fever.' Charlotte was unusually vehement, 'We work at the bedside, we are practical human beings and are horrified by the malicious ignorance of those so-called top men who not only attack you but all the mothers of the world.'

'Ignaz, she is right, you are right and I shall do everything in my power to ensure your work and its practical life-saving value is recognised.' Markusovszky's loyalty and scientific insight cheered his friend.

'It is only because of you all,' he looked in turn at Maria, Lajos and Charlotte and finally his new daughter, 'that I do not become more depressed.'

One month later Semmelweis wrote two open letters to the *Vienna Medical Weekly*. His passion and self belief clearly showed through. Addressing Professor Späth, newly appointed Professor of Midwifery in Vienna in 1861, he said, 'The puerperal sun rose in Vienna in 1847 but closed minds have not been lit. As a result many women have died and you, Herr Professor, have participated in this massacre.' Turning to Professor Scanzoni he unleashed a furious attack. 'Due to ignorance of my statistics you have indulged in murderous practice. The time will come, I feel certain, when, to put it mildly, you will feel sorry that you can no longer blot out from the memory of people the fact that you were the first to oppose my views on puerperal fever.'

Lajos Markusovszky discussed the strong language with Semmelweis. 'You realise, Ignaz, that people might question your sanity; this would be their way of protecting themselves.'

'I know, Lajos, but the groaning of dying lying-in women is louder than the beating of my heart. I have been obstructed by ignorance, vanity and indifference – all they had to do was wash their hands.'

'We all understand and endorse your teachings but as you well know being in the right makes you vulnerable to those with most to lose.'

'I know, I know,' there was a hint of irritability in his voice.

Semmelweis was further wounded, when in October 1861 he was not invited to a meeting at Speyer in south-west Germany attended by a wide variety of German specialists. He was roundly attacked in his absence by everyone present with the single exception of Professor Wilhelm Lange of Heidelberg. Rudolf Virchow again doubted Semmelweis' methodology.

The following year Lajos Markusovszky answered every single critic, point by point, in the *Vienna Medical Weekly*. This raised Semmelweis' spirits once again and he was further buoyed up by the birth of his son, Bela, on 20 November 1862.

Time passed. Semmelweis remained silent but gradually acceptance of chlorine hand washing increased and by 1864 was routine practice in Zurich, Hanover, Pest and Saint Petersburg.

His home life was a source of great happiness and on

26 July his second daughter, Antónia, was born. He continued his routine work performing gynaecological and obstetric operations to both his satisfaction and the approval of his patients and colleagues. There were times, particularly when he read of further criticism, that he was seen to be irritable and a little difficult to please.

Lajos Markusovszky arranged to meet Charlotte at a restaurant in Pest in early March 1865. They had become Semmelweis' closest friends and had, of course, followed his fight against childbed fever and bigoted colleagues for the past twenty years. They were concerned about the monumental stress this had placed on him.

'Of course,' said Charlotte, 'he was greatly encouraged by Professor Späth's open letter from Vienna at the end of last year.'

'At long last,' Lajos sighed, 'Vienna has chlorine hand washing. It was a huge turn around for him to confess that no physician can reject Semmelweis' doctrine.'

'Nevertheless, when I see him during visits to the children I find him fragile.'

'He still needs us – you, me and Maria,' Markusovszky was worried. 'His depression is a normal human reaction to the serious onslaught he has endured. We still have our self-appointed job.' He smiled at her.

47

Final Curtain

At eight o'clock on the morning of 3 July 1865 Professor Ignaz Semmelweis made a skin incision in the abdomen of a forty-nine-year-old woman who had been admitted to the gynaecology ward the previous evening. She had, according to her husband, complained of pain in the lower belly for three days. One day after this she became distended, vomited all she took by mouth and developed a high fever. Examination had shown her to be pale, sweating and she had rapid, shallow respiration. The abdomen was hugely distended in the lower part and there was a foul, thick, greenish-brown vaginal discharge.

Ignaz and his team diagnosed an acute gynaecological surgical emergency. All attempts to quell her fever with cold compresses and quench her thirst with water had failed.

'We have to operate,' explained Semmelweis to his assistant, Dr Tibor Németh, 'or else she would most certainly be dead by this evening,' his voice was cheerful and he sounded optimistic. 'Let's see what's inside.' He held up the peritoneal lining of the abdominal cavity with two pairs of forceps. 'Make a small incision here,' he pointed to the tented-up membrane.

'Yes, sir,' Tibor was a little nervous in the presence of his famous chief. He made a small opening and instantly offensive-smelling green fluid flooded out under great pressure. He withdrew the blade abruptly and accidentally made a small wound on the third finger of Professor Semmelweis' ungloved right hand. There was a little bleeding, a nurse wiped the cut with a cloth soaked in chlorine hand wash and there was no further mention of the incident during the remainder of the procedure.

The doctors found a massive abscess of the left fallopian tube and ovary which had ruptured into the peritoneal cavity. Pus was widespread and loops of intestine were bound together, forming multiple pockets of a green gelatinous substance. The fetid material was cleaned out, irrigation with saline performed, the ovarian remnants removed and the wound in the belly partly closed to allow free drainage into bulky linen dressings.

'She has a good chance now,' the anaesthetist said, as he started to bring her round.

During the following three days the patient steadily improved; she kept down water and her fever abated. Semmelweis' finger remained sore and was a little red. He experienced one or two shivering attacks. Maria asked if he was all right, 'It's nothing, I'm fine,' he replied irritably. She let it pass.

However, one week later, on 13 July, Maria Semmelweis noticed a sudden definite change in her husband. He became very restless. That night he did not go to bed and paced from room to room arguing with his unseen opponents, 'You are not doctors but murderers; you are pompous, self-important and ignorant, the desperation to preserve your petty reputations blinds you to the truth.'

The next morning, having had no sleep, he attended an appointments committee meeting to select a new lecturer in his own department. When the first candidate was seated Ignaz stood up and withdrew a crumpled piece of paper from his waistcoat pocket. He unfolded it with shaking hands and read, 'God Almighty, the Father, the Son and Holy Spirit, the whole trinity, the eternal God being my help in my everlasting belief that I have been called by the head of the town of Nagykálló for the task of a midwife—' increasingly he stumbled and faltered over the words.

This passage was from an ancient oath produced by the Calvinist church in the small town of Nagykálló, near the city of Nyíregyháza in north-east Hungary.

These were the last words spoken in public by Ignaz Phillip Semmelweis, professor of theoretical and practical obstetrics in the Royal Hungarian University of Pest.

His friends and colleagues could clearly see he was ill. János Balassa and the paediatrician János Bókay went to his side and gently took hold of each trembling arm. 'Come, Ignaz,' said Balassa, 'let us go home to Maria.'

For the next two weeks Balassa, Markusovszky, Charlotte and Maria tried to help him, but his deterioration continued. On one occasion he was found in a dishevelled state near the bank of the Danube haranguing a group of incredulous bystanders, 'You have abandoned the truth, more lying-in women will die.' They helped him home once again.

'What is wrong with him?' Maria asked Lajos.

'I think poison from his cut finger has got into his bloodstream and is affecting his brain.'

'What can we do?'

'He may need professional care.' He produced the latest copy of *Vienna Medical Weekly*, dated 18 July 1865. In it was Ignaz' paper, 'Operative Treatment of Ovarian Cysts'. Semmelweis stared blankly at his own work and tossed it to the floor.

The deterioration continued, with irrational behaviour and sleep disturbed nights. On 31 July, Balassa, Markusovszky and Bókay had no alternative – they certified their patient as temporarily insane.

'Maria, there is an excellent psychiatrist at the lower Austrian mental home. Dr Hofrath Riedel has an excellent reputation,' Markusovszky continued, 'he knew Ignaz at medical school and I think he will give us the best possibility of an early cure. It will, of course, be preferable for him personally, professionally and for the university to seek to restore him to health at a distance from Budapest.'

Later the same day a docile Semmelweis, Maria, their two daughters and son, Markusovszky and Charlotte set off on the four-hour train journey from Budapest to Vienna.

On arrival they were met by Ferdinand Von Hebra. He embraced Ignaz, 'My poor dear friend,' he saw no trace of recognition from his long time colleague. The party proceeded by coach to the lunatic asylum only to find that Dr Riedel was on holiday. His deputy, Dr Mildner, admitted the unfortunate obstetrician to the ward for maniacs. In his medical record he includes a note of the unhealed, inflamed laceration of the middle finger of his patient's right hand.

During his first night in the institution Semmelweis was delirious and attempted to escape from the building. 'He was so violent,' alleged one of the burly attendants, 'it required six of us to restrain him.' Six huge, strong young men to control a frail, malnourished, confused, middle-aged and emaciated doctor.

The seriously ill man remained withdrawn, taking little food and drink, but when two days later Dr Riedel returned and hurried to see his old colleague, Semmelweis lashed out at him. It was the custom in those days to put such a person in a canvas strait-jacket and he was immobilised.

He was judged to be sufficiently subdued on 11 August and the cruel restraint was removed. Semmelweis was barely conscious and his left elbow was so badly ulcerated by his struggling in his bondage that the joint was exposed and full of pus. The red and black swollen inflammation extended up to his shoulder and the lymph glands in the axilla were massive and discharging dark blood-stained fluid.

Professor Ignaz Phillip Semmelweis died at eleven o'clock on the morning of 13 August 1865. He was forty-seven years of age. The notice handed to his wife Maria stated that the cause of death was paralysis of the brain.

The funeral ceremony took place at the Vienna General hospital 15 August. Maria, holding one-year-old Antónia in her arms, stood at the front with the tiny figures of Magrit and Béla at her side. Surrounding her were the assembled staff, doctors, nurses, orderlies and administrators of the hospital. Included in this large silent gathering were Professors Rokitanski, Skoda, Späth and Von Hebra.

Lajos Markusovszky gave the address. He spoke of a kind, gentle, intelligent friend, horrified by the suffering of lying-in women who contracted childbed fever. He described the dedicated research leading to Semmelweis' discovery of the cause and prevention of this terrible disease. He told of Semmelweis' struggle to make his voice heard in a hostile medical world. He spoke of the warmth of Ignaz' family and friends. He concluded by quoting a foreign but well-known poet.

> March sadly after; grace my mourning here
> In weeping after, this untimely bier.

Standing a little to one side of the main group was a grateful but sad midwife holding tightly on to the hand of her twenty-two-year-old daughter. They were accompanied by an elegant tall elderly gentleman, two young women, a handsome man and an elderly pleasant-looking lady. They turned as one and slowly walked away.

207

Epilogue

A post-mortem examination of the body of Ignaz Semmelweis was performed in the Vienna General Hospital shortly after his death and the report appeared in the *Vienna Medical Weekly*. It confirmed the unhealed wound of his right middle finger and gangrene of the left elbow. Most of the major organs, including the brain, were affected by inflammatory swelling, exudates and abscess formation. There was no conclusive evidence of long-standing disease of the central nervous system.

Semmelweis was accused of madness by his detractors before and after death. There is no reason to doubt that, in later years, he suffered from intermittent episodes of depression. Nevertheless, any normal, sensitive human being is bound to experience a degree of depression in response to repeated verbal and published abuse.

His final illness is reasonably explained by the finger that was accidentally cut, becoming infected during that fateful last operation. It led to a low-grade septicaemia causing an organic psychosis. Three weeks later his gangren-ous left elbow gave rise to an overwhelming fulminating pyaemia resulting in multiple organ failure and death.

Lajos Markusovszky continued vigorously to champion his friend's teaching and became one of the greatest contributors to scientific medicine in the second half of the nineteenth century. He lived to see the general acceptance of Semmelweis' work in Germany and elsewhere after the publication of confirmatory statistics in 1886. He died seven years later.

Rudolf Virchow had, as a young man, made a notable impact on medicine with his book on cellular pathology but persisted in his personal and professional opposition to Semmelweis' views into cantankerous old age.

In 1867 Lord Lister gave his first account of the antiseptic carbolic treatment of wounds and in 1879 Louis Pasteur announced the discovery of bacteria causing puerperal fever.

The Pest Institute of Obstetrics and Gynaecology no longer exists but the Saint Rochus Hospital endured and flourishes to this day. A fine statue of Semmelweis with a poor woman expressing gratitude stands outside. It was unveiled in 1906 at a ceremony attended by Maria, who died four years later. In Hungary, 15 July is the Day of the Medical Profession and each year doctors and nurses from the Saint Rochus Hospital place flowers on the memorial.

1956 saw Russian tanks on the streets of Budapest in response to a democratically elected government proclaiming independence. Imre Nagy, the reforming leader, together with thousands of supporters was executed. There was massive bloodshed and many of the injured were taken to the Saint Rochus Hospital. Sador Pomersein, the chief surgeon at that time, worked tirelessly treating the victims. He gained spiritual strength in the adjoining church.

The winds of *perestroika* swept away the Soviet regime in 1990. Today Hungary is a free democratic republic with a beautiful capital city.

Appendix

The Aetiology, Concept and Prophylaxis of Childbed Fever

Semmelweis accepted from the outset that such a long title to a book daunted the average medical reader, let alone the intended lay person. Nevertheless he felt this was his first and probably last opportunity to tell the full story in scientific detail. He selected the words carefully and judged them to be a precise description of the important points in his message.

In a short Preface he describes the complexities of his appointment in Vienna. He states that his object is to present his observations and doubts about the current teachings concerning the origin and concept of childbed fever. Asserting his aversion to polemics and controversy, he expresses his disappointment that after thirteen years he has not seen the truth triumph over its detractors and therefore is being forced to write the book. The preface is dated, 'Pest, 30 August 1860'.

The first chapter is an autobiographical introduction, which opens with the words, 'Medicine's highest duty is saving threatened human life and obstetrics is the branch of medicine in which this duty is most obviously fulfilled'. There follows a description of the obstetric scene that opens up to him on his arrival at the Vienna General Hospital.

He focuses on the high incidence of childbed fever with its appalling death rate for mothers and babies and the terrible suffering of the lying-in women. He gives a detailed account of the adverse conditions that existed in the obstetric clinics.

He follows this with an account of the various theories held by top men in the centres of excellence throughout Europe. He notes the particular emphasis on atmospheric influences, and states that this scourge is the fate of these poor women. He is unable to accept any of these assumptions.

He notes the comparatively low incidence of childbed fever in the second obstetric clinic where midwives receive instruction, compared with the first clinic, where medical students are taught. He comments on the fact that medical students assist at autopsies and that for midwives this is not part of their training.

The observations prompt him to undertake a detailed statistical analysis of all births at the Vienna General Hospital since its opening in 1789. This is a massive undertaking, trawling through the dusty archives of over 200,000 births.

As it slowly dawns on him, he is horrified that these pioneering statistics clearly demonstrate a connection between autopsies on the victims of puerperal fever and mortality from this terrible disease in the first obstetric clinic. He himself is involved.

He chronicles the physical and mental exhaustion he experiences from both his research and the antagonism he experiences throughout the profession. His account tells of his uplifting visit to Venice and the key role of Professor Jakob Kolletschka, both alive and dead.

His second chapter deals with the concept of childbed fever. This entails defining what it is not, as well as what it is. He carefully excludes epidemic and atmospheric theories by using the smallpox analogy: smallpox causes only smallpox in previously healthy individuals.

Logically he then surveys the vast number of endemic factors that exist both in the patient's circumstances and the hospital environment. Since the hospital was free and the mothers in return served a teaching role many were poor, deprived and malnourished, indeed some had come after the unsuccessful attentions of an abortionist, but these considerations operated equally in both the first and second obstetric clinics. Curiously, those unfortunate women who gave birth en route to the hospital but had still not passed the placenta were less affected. They were known as street births.

There were many factors within the hospital, conditions that could have played a part in puerperal fever. These included dampness, overcrowding and even the priest with his bell, but again these applied equally to both clinics.

Semmelweis then turns his attention to the question of contagious origins of the puerperal scourge.

This had been an attractive theory, that one person developed the disease following contact with another. However, it does not explain why only women who were recently delivered were the ones to be affected nor the difference in the occurrence of childbed fever in the first obstetric clinic compared with the second unit. For example, a woman suffering from the disease who comes in contact with a woman who has not recently been delivered of an infant does not give the same condition to her.

Of course men do not contract childbed fever from an affected woman but, as the case of Kolletschka showed, similar post-mortem changes may be seen in men and babies but without the genital areas being affected.

Semmelweis then turns his attention to internal and external factors. He uses the term internal to refer to

212

those rare circumstances where decaying organic matter exists within the pregnant woman before delivery. Examples are the death of a foetus before the onset of labour and the coincidental development of potentially fatal conditions, such as appendicitis, in a pregnant woman.

Finally he looks at external influences based on his clinical, statistical and post-mortem studies. He says, 'I maintain that puerperal fever is an absorption fever, produced by the absorption of decomposing animal or organic material. Puerperal fever is not a specific disease, but a variety of pyaemia.' Through the circulating blood numerous organs may be affected to varying degrees with abscesses and effusions. He concludes that the decaying organic material is carried by the examining fingers, the operating hand, contaminated linen, instruments, sponges and bedpans. This material is then introduced into the damaged, bruised, torn and vulnerable genitalia of the recently delivered mother.

In the following chapter he demonstrates by extensive statistical evidence that this dead or decaying organic material is transferred by doctors and medical students from autopsies to the lying-in women.

Chapter Four briefly reconsiders the endemic factors, which he had previously excluded during his examination of the epidemic theories.

The fifth chapter discusses chlorine hand washing to prevent childbed fever. He shows the dramatic reduction of childbed fever as a result of this procedure, particularly in the first obstetric clinic of the Vienna General Hospital.

Feeling strongly that vast numbers of lives can be saved he uses forceful and dogmatic language stating that the transfer of decaying organic material to the genitalia of lying-in women is the only cause of puerperal fever. He appeals to all governments to make chlorine hand washing compulsory by law and says, 'This is in order that life yet unborn will not be infected with seeds of death by those very persons who are called to protect life'.

In his enthusiasm to put his discovery into practice his words become even more extravagant and he lets slip into his account, 'fool', 'evil'; 'fallacious teaching', 'death reaping a rich harvest', 'pernicious behaviour', 'misled physicians', and 'decimation of the childbearing sex'.

His strength of feeling is shown in the passage: 'My doctrines are not for gathering dust in libraries but are a practical guide for all doctors, including the village general practitioner and district midwife', and he finishes philosophically, 'to preserve the wife for her husband and mother for her child'.

The sixth and final chapter in his book is devoted to the reactions to his teachings throughout Europe. Initially, he turns his attention to his detractors.

Karl Braun continued to deny the value of chlorine hand washing, which was abandoned in Vienna, and in 1854 there were over 400 deaths from childbed fever. It is incredible to think that pique and pettiness could form the basis for such action. He had failed to become professor of obstetrics in Pest.

Likewise, Wilhelm Scanzoni, who was by now professor of obstetrics in Würzburg, persists in his epidemic theory in the face of overwhelming evidence from Semmelweis to the contrary.

Most hurtful of all are the words of Rudolf Virchow, professor of pathological anatomy in Berlin. This man, widely respected throughout Europe for his book *Cellular Pathology* had revolutionised knowledge of disease by showing specific changes in cells. He was methodical but not driven to introduce practical measures to save lives. He says, 'Natural science knows no bugbears other than persons, who speculate'. Semmelweis believes this is speculation.

There are, however numerous supporters of Ignaz' chlorine hand washing, these obstetricians confirm its value both at meetings and in print. They include Charles Routh at the Samaritan Free Hospital in London, the late Gustav Michaelis in Kiel and Christian Tilanus in Amsterdam.

Semmelweis feels wounded but vindicated and writes in his Epilogue,

> When with my current convictions, I look into the past, I can endure the miseries to which I have been subjected only by looking at the same time into the future; I see a time when only cases of self infection will occur in the maternity hospitals of the world. In comparison with the great numbers thus to be saved in the future, the number of patients saved by my students and by me is insignificant. If I am not allowed to see this fortunate time with my own eyes, therefore, my death will nevertheless be brightened by the conviction that sooner or later this time will inevitably arrive.

Glossary

Abdomen	Part of the body containing stomach, intestines, liver and reproductive organs etc, also called belly, tummy. The internal lining is the peritoneum.
Abscess	A focus of infection containing pus, usually due to bacteria.
Absorption	Penetration of a lining membrane.
Aetiology	Factors causing a disease.
Amnion	Membrane surrounding the foetus.
Aspirant lecturer	A post held before becoming a professor.
Autopsy post-mortem	Examination of a body after death.
Bacterium	A single cell micro-organism sometimes causing disease.
Bacteraemia	Bacteria in the bloodstream. *Septicaemia* – Infection with multiplying bacteria in the bloodstream. *Pyaemia* – Pus in the bloodstream.
Breech	Delivery of baby with buttocks and feet first.
Cadaver	Corpse – dead body.
Cancer	Malignant invasive tumour with uncontrolled cell division – fatal if untreated.
Cell	Nucleus, cytoplasm and membrane – basis of life.

Cervix	Neck of the womb (uterus) – dilates during birth process leading to the *vagina* (birth canal), opening into the *vulva*. Together with the two ovaries producing eggs and hormones and fallopian tubes conveying eggs (*ova*) to the uterus, these structures are known as the female genitalia or reproductive organs.
Childbed	Childbirth
Chlorine	Chemical element, a gas, passed through water to form *Liquida Chlorina*, combined with a compound of calcium to form chloride of lime (calcium hypochlorite), destroys bacteria.
Cleft lip	Developmental defect in the upper lip.
Clerk	Taking a history, examining and making a diagnosis of a patient recorded in handwritten notes.
Cord	Umbilical, joins foetus and newborn child to the placenta carrying blood.
Cosmic	Of the universe. *Miasma* – noxious vapours. *Telluric* – of the planet earth.
Crisis	Turning point of a fever.
Cyst	Sac with fluid contents.
Decay/ Decompose	Breakdown of dead tissue by bacteria.
Delirium	Acute mental disorder involving incoherent speech, hallucinations, frenzied excitement, usually associated with toxic, febrile or metabolic conditions.
Depression	Extreme dejection and hopelessness. Endogenous from within with no apparent cause or reactive to events.
Differential diagnosis	List in order of probability of the possible diagnosis.
Discharge	Pouring out of fluid, often pus, from a part of the body.

Effusion	Outpouring of fluid, usually into a body cavity.
Engaged	In obstetrics, when during labour the baby's head enters the bony pelvis of the mother.
Engorged	Congested with blood.
External	(factors causing disease) – from outside the patient. *Internal* – from within the patient. *Endemic* – from the immediate environment. *Epidemic* – from the atmosphere. *Contagious* – from direct contact with another patient.
Exudate	Escape of fluid containing protein from a body surface.
Fasciculus	Bundle of fibres.
Fever/febrile	Above normal body temperature.
Fibrin	Protein in blood and exudates.
Foetus	Unborn child.
Forceps	Surgical instrument for holding tissues. Obstetric – for holding the baby's head.
Forensic	Of or used in courts of law.
Fulminating	Sudden and overwhelming.
Gangrene	Death of tissue due to obstruction of arterial blood supply and therefore oxygen.
Glacis	Slope on outside of city or fort wall.
Gloves	Surgical rubber – introduced after 1870.
Grand Round	Weekly meeting for teaching involving the whole staff and students of a professorial clinical department.
Gripe/colic	Spasmodic pain due to muscle in the wall of a hollow organ contracting to expel an obstruction.
Hyperinosis	Increased fibrin in blood.
Hypothesis	Supposition made as a starting point for further investigation.

Ichor	Mythical fluid flowing in veins of gods.
Inflammation	Reaction to injury or infection – hot, red, swollen, painful.
Intra-uterine death	Death of foetus in the uterus.
Labour	Process of childbirth
Laceration	A cut.
Lateral	(position) lying on one side. *Dorsal* – lying on back.
Laudanum	Solution containing morphine – powerful painkiller.
Lochia	Discharge from uterus after childbirth.
Lying-in	Period of recovery after childbirth.
Lymphatics	System of glands and vessels containing clear fluid with white cells involved in the body's defences.
Lymphangitis	Infection with bacteria spreading through lymphatics.
Mal-presentation	A part of the baby's body that is not the head at the cervix. Breech, transverse.
Manual expression	Pressure on the abdomen to force out the placenta.
Membrane	Sheet-like covering or lining of an organ.
Metastasis	Transfer from one organ to another.
Midwife	A nurse trained to assist women in childbirth.
MRSA	Methicillin resistant staphylococcus aureus.
Myomectomy	Removing a fibroid (muscle tumour) from the uterus.
Obstetrics	Branch of medicine concerned with childbirth.
Olfactory	Related to smell.
Orderly	Semi-skilled hospital worker.

Organic	Structures of the body.
	Chemistry – of carbon
	Decaying organic material – dead animal matter.
	Psychosis – severe mental derangement due to brain disease, e.g. tumour, septicaemia.
Pathology	Science of diseased organs of the body.
Pericarditis	Infection around the heart within its covering membrane (pericardium).
Peritonitis	Inflammation of the peritoneum – lining the inside of the abdomen.
Pharmacology	Science of actions of drugs on the body.
Phlebitis	Inflammation of a vein.
Phlogistic	Mythical cause of combustion.
Placenta	Flat circular organ attached to the wall of the uterus nourishing the foetus via the umbilical cord.
Plague	Previously fatal disease spread via rat fleas to humans.
Pleurisy	Inflammation of the pleura (membrane) lining the chest and lungs.
Polemic	Controversial discussion.
Postgraduate	Further study after obtaining university degree.
Premature	Foetus before full development of forty weeks.
Professor	Head of university department, responsible for teaching and research.
Prophylaxis	Prevention of disease.
Puerperal	Of childbirth.
Purge	Empty the intestines.
Pus	Thick yellow or green liquid produced by infected tissue containing white blood cells, bacteria and debris.

Putrid	Decomposed.
Rigor	Fever with shivering.
Rotation	Manually changing the position of the foetus to the correct position.
Rupture	Burst.
Scabies	Irritating skin disease due to burrowing mite.
Sepsis	Contamination with bacteria.
Smallpox	Contagious viral disease causing skin pustules.
Street birth	Birth outside of building.
Suppurate	Form pus.
Therapeutics	Treatment of disease.
Tissue	Collection of specialised cells forming an organ.
Toxic	Poisonous.
Transverse (lie)	Foetus lying horizontally in the uterus.
Tuberculosis	Infectious bacterial disease usually affects lungs but may involve any other structure in the body.
Ulcer	Break in a body surface.
Venereal disease	Sexually transmitted disease.
Waters	(breaking) – rupture of the amniotic sac releasing fluid causing or accelerating labour.
Wet nurse	Woman breast-feeding another's child.